Mansion Dreams

Mansion Dreams

A NOVEL

Barbara Shorr

Mill City Press, Inc.
322 First Avenue N, 5th floor
Minneapolis, MN 55401
612.455.2293
www.millcitypublishing.com

ISBN-13: 978-1-63413-478-1
LCCN: 2015905748

Cover Design by Barbara Shorr
Typeset by MK Ross
Photo by Lisa Richman

Printed in the United States of America

Acknowledgments

Many thanks to my editor, Elizabeth Barrett, for her significant insights on story development and manuscript preparation. A special thank you to my friend and writer, Barbara J. Klinger, who read the original draft of *Mansion Dreams* and suggested that I work toward publication. Thanks also to the members of the Palm Beach Writers Group for welcoming this new writer and sharing their publication experiences.

Most of all, I wish to thank my husband, Bernard, for his unfailing encouragement, advice, and especially patience throughout the process.

Prologue

April 1994

Two years had passed since Merry Dawn Venture hit the big four-o, and once again she celebrated by tossing a handful of confetti in the air. As the bits of colored paper floated down over her, creating meaningless kaleidoscopic designs on the carpet, she mused, *A scattered mess.* This was an observation of her reality: the patterns of her life were as aimless as the random patterns of confetti as it drifted onto the carpet.

So this was it. Her life. The way it was. Her annual ritual continued as she scooped the confetti from the carpet and deposited the colored bits of paper into a small white envelope for next year. *Do the math, kid,* she told herself. *Do the math. You're over forty. What have you got to show for it?*

Her life was the result of choices, not lack of opportunities. It was far safer for Merry to stand before the closed doors of chance than to open one and perhaps change her life. After all, it was probably all she deserved; was what she deserved. Who was she anyway? It was easier to be consoled with the vague promise that maybe, one day, things would change—as if the sky would open and drop something wonderful at her feet. A timid woman's prayer, a fool's wish—the universal fantasy of a lingering adolescence, hidden behind the beginning of a jowl.

How strange, given that she allowed the opportunities that paraded by to escape, as if she were oblivious to everything around her but the comfort and security of her job at La Viola. It was her lifeline in an otherwise fearful, wasted, and lonely existence.

Merry's acquaintances, as she did not have or encourage close friendships, were also on the other side of the big four-o. Unlike Merry, they took a more pragmatic view of their chosen—or "temporarily unavoidable"—situations and made remedial corrections. They took lovers as necessary parts of their lives—as necessary as their cosmetic surgeries, which transformed them into wide-eyed twenty-year-olds with forty-plus bodies. With their hair just a tad gray under frosted roots, they resembled molting owls searching for prey.

On occasional evenings, they met for dinner and drinks at trendy Upper East Side restaurants. Each one would take a turn singing her aria of the plights of single life. One bemoaned that her life stank, another bitched about her job, and the martyr of the group proclaimed that she was standing by her latest lover, even if he was going through a rough period of adjustment (her oblique reference to not having had sex for, well, months, but hey, what else was out there?). All agreed that there were three types of men available for women over "a certain age"—divorced, diseased, or dying. Then, fueled by a couple or three drinks, Shellie, Gloria, and Caprice always ended these evenings in crescendos of laughter. Merry just sat and listened.

"The trouble is, he thinks the big bang theory applies to his sex life. You know—do it once and that's it. Maybe it's some kind of male menopause. But with him, it's not just a pause. Do you think he's having an affair?"

Eyes met, flashed, and rolled. "Why, sweetie, whatever would cause you to think that?"

An evening of whine and wine. No one took it seriously except Merry, whose voyeuristic yearnings placed her within these narratives. No one ever asked her what she was doing. They all knew. Nothing. Yet whenever their occasional evenings were planned, they included Merry, because all agreed that here was one lonely woman, a woman they most likely would not have noticed in a crowd, but they happened to be clients of the decorator shop she managed.

Although disparate, each woman had a timetable for her ride to success: education with a goal toward a career and, most of all, becoming financially independent.

It was a coincidence that all three women were at La Viola Interiors on the same Saturday, allowing themselves a pillow splurge. For women who spent little time in their homes, their apartments were exquisitely appointed. Only the best. They treated themselves well because they could afford it. They started to meet after that—not often, every couple of months. But their individual relationships with Merry were different. Each woman realized that lonely Merry could be a conduit for her secrets. It was like confiding to a stranger you met in an airport waiting area when your plane was three hours late. What difference did it make? Whom would Merry tell? Confessing to Merry was catharsis minus the analyst fee.

Merry looked into the bottom of her second glass of Chardonnay as if the answer to her secret, nagging question would float up. *Will there ever be someone in my life?*

For a moment, she imagined seeing an answer: *It's up to you.*

One

The apartment looked as if Merry was in the process of moving in or moving out. Wallpaper and fabric sample books lingered against the walls with the pathetic neglect of ignored wallflowers at a dance. Even the Venetian blinds, which had come with the apartment, slouched unevenly on the windows, resembling a slovenly neighbor hanging over the sill, looking for something—anything—to happen. The furniture, left by the previous occupants, had a distinct look of hand-wringing despair. The lumpy seat cushion resembled a flabby body sprawled on the sofa. Shoeboxes and shopping bags crowded the tiny bedroom, which was dominated by an unmade bed—the kind that suggested the late-night thrashing of its lone occupant. A jar of instant coffee, an electric wine cooler, a box with two stale donuts, and a plastic dish containing some overripe grapes accessorized the otherwise barren galley kitchen. In the bathroom, a hairdryer and an electric toothbrush rested on the top of the toilet tank. This was her home, the apartment in the back of a building with a cachet address. Off Fifth Avenue. East Side. Walking distance from Museum Mile.

In contrast to the funereal gloom of her neglected apartment, Merry crafted an external image of a fashion plate. What she spent on her clothes could furnish an eight-room apartment. Perhaps an exaggeration, but clothes, she reasoned, were important to her professional life. Still she wore them with no more sentiment or enthusiasm or personal flair than a department-store window mannequin.

Merry's work world was the alter ego of her otherwise uneventful existence; the two comprised the aspects of the inner and the outer Merry. From her early beginnings managing the Manhattan branch of the La Viola Second Avenue interior decor studio to her move to the new Madison Avenue location, Merry was a success, catering to career women who were too insecure to pick out a throw pillow. When she gave her blessings to a fabric swatch, nodded with approval at a duvet, or guided a client to the perfect sofa style, the client always splurged and went over budget, "just this once." When Merry heard that a rival decorator described the showroom as "Bronx Renaissance colliding with Brooklyn Baroque and tied up in a fringed velvet straitjacket," she thought it was so funny, she reworded the quip and had it needlepointed on throw pillows: "Neoclassic and abstract never clash when you're the one who's got the cash." All three dozen sold out in two weeks, even the ones without fringe.

Most evenings, Merry stuck to her afterwork ritual of a frozen dinner, a glass of wine, and a quick shower. Then, pulling on her old belted cotton flannel jacket and jeans—twenty-year-old relics but too comfy to discard— and a pair of well-worn fuzzy slippers, she curled up on the sofa to work on proposals and contracts while all around her hummed the vibrant city, filled with more possibilities for human experience than the stars in the heavens.

Manhattan, the Big Apple, *the* city. Museums, theaters, and art galleries, each featuring a daily inexhaustible galaxy of offerings for new experiences. Yet Merry's was a life imposed like a punishment without a crime. It was more comfortable to shut everything out than to face the nagging, unformed fear of anticipated disappointment.

One November evening around ten, the ring of the telephone pierced the silence that usually dominated Merry's apartment. On the second ring, she picked up the receiver, and before she could say hello, she heard that familiar voice.

"Merry, where have you been?"

That warm, teasing masculine voice always set off a cascade of ambivalent emotions whenever he called, which was infrequently. How long had it been since he last called? Merry tried to gather her composure and, mustering up her most casual voice, responded, "I could say the same to you, Randy Grant." She put her paperwork aside.

There was that awkward silence as she tried to think of what to say next. She failed. So for that short span of time, which seemed like an eternity, she felt her heart beating, if not pounding, to that nagging, unidentified feeling that arose at the sound of Randy's voice.

"I've had a few changes in my life since I last saw you." Randy's voice had the tone of saying one thing but meaning something else. No matter what he said, Merry chose to perceive the warmth of his voice as the sound of seduction, which, for Randy, was not intended and certainly would not happen.

"Like what? Trying to find yourself with some twenty-year-old?" *Why don't I just say what I mean?* This was punctuated by a nervous giggle and a strange feeling of being both hot and cold, as she kept shifting her position on the sofa, from curling up to stretching out to sitting bolt upright. But Merry continued the conversation, back and forth with Randy, like the precise beat of a metronome.

"Not twenty," he said. "Someone more mature." That teasing voice again.

"So you got dumped." *I wish he'd be a little less casual and stop taking me for granted.*

"Nothing like that, I can assure you. Besides, I generally like them older, around twenty and a half."

"Doesn't your boyish charm work for you anymore?" Merry stretched out again on the sofa, preparing for their typical wisecracking conversations, which usually went nowhere.

"Always a remark from you." His voice suggested a slight rebuke and then, after a pause, took on a casual air, as if he just remembered something he wanted to say. "By the way, I'm going to England for a few weeks. How about getting together tomorrow after work for a drink at my place?"

"What do you want to do? See how I compare with your last prospect?" *Is it Randy or me?* Merry wondered. They always seemed to ride the same conversational treadmill.

"Come over around seven. And there will be no comparisons of anything."

"I'll be there, but don't serve me any cocktail franks. I'm off little weenies." *Why had I said that? All I had to do was accept the invitation and let it go at that.*

"Very funny."

With that, he hung up, ending the conversation as he always did—when he wanted to. Merry never had the chance to hang up first. She could not penetrate that Randy persona. But then, she always acted glib, as if everything he said required some kind of a comeback, which she knew Randy took to mean she was just someone who was fun to talk with when he wasn't otherwise occupied.

He liked Merry but could not figure her out. There was something hidden about her, as if she were holding out and keeping her true self from emerging. Merry, he concluded, was not like ice, which could be melted, but like a brick wall—impenetrable.

Still, she accepted the vagaries of their longtime relationship, welcoming Randy's occasional calls. He treated her as he treated all his friends and acquaintances: in a carefree and casual manner that kept him at a respectable arm's length from emotional entanglement. Merry never questioned herself about this good-buddy relationship. She liked his company, infrequent as it was, yet she always felt on edge about something in herself. *What makes me feel this way?* she wondered. *Come on, I haven't time to think about this. I have work to do.*

But Merry was losing her resolve to concentrate on style numbers and pattern choices. It was a struggle, lost in a myriad of conflicting thoughts and emotions. *What have I done to myself? I'm so alone, and I don't know what to do. What if I tried to be warmer? No, I can't risk that. What if…*

A large tear splashed on the order form. Then a torrent of tears gushed from her eyes, and the steely, chill feeling of hollow, empty loneliness swept over her as she got up and looked out the window. The view of the back of the neighboring building formed a well of darkness, with the exception of a single light glimmering from one of the apartments. Suddenly, the light shut off, leaving her alone in her dark misery. Merry took a deep breath, exhaled, and pulled the jacket belt tightly around herself. She walked into her bedroom, threw herself on her unmade bed, and fell asleep.

By eight o'clock the next morning, Merry was in her office, immersed in a busy day of seeing clients, writing proposals, ordering fabrics, and confirming appointments. While drinking her midmorning coffee, she thought about the walk over to see Randy that evening. Those two short blocks might as well have led her to another planet. A year's time had separated them, the verbal sparring partners. He didn't call. She forgot to call. They had mix-ups about where they were supposed to meet; silly arguments but no apologies. Two adults behaving like undisciplined children. Yet for all their ups and downs, when they did get together, they were always able to pick up where they left off. One time, Randy went off suddenly to see clients in Europe. No good-bye. One month passed. Two months. Hearing nothing, Merry indulged her needy imagination, and in a dramatic moment of pretending that perhaps…Humoring herself about a romance that never was, but still, if she had only… Merry bought a little silver charm in the shape of a teardrop. She wore it once.

The office phone rang. She let the answering machine turn on. "Merry, it's me-e-e-e! Call me at the magazine. Bet you can't guess what I found out." Click.

Merry wasn't in the mood for guessing. It was either something Caprice thought she'd heard, or better yet, something she knew had been omitted from a piece of gossip.

"It's always best to get some kind of confirmation," Caprice would say. "Why spread rumors if you don't know the facts? It's so tacky." She was thoughtful that way.

Merry called back.

"Okay, Cappy, this better be something good." Merry always continued working when talking on the phone with Caprice, who was the champion nonstop talker of all things important to Cappy.

"Well, remember when we were leaving Nicola's last week? I heard Shellie telling you that she was going to get 'so tight that—' but the taxi pulled up, and I couldn't hear her. Do you know what she was talking about?"

Cappy always said exactly what was on her mind, but she sounded as if she had just thought of what to say at that very moment. There was a tremor of surprise in her voice, as if what she had blurted out was amazing—as if the thought had come from somewhere else.

"Me? No, I haven't a clue." Merry addressed an envelope and stuffed in a contract.

"Wanna meet for lunch?" The way Cappy asked the question, it sounded conspiratorial.

"What time and where?"

"I'll call you around noon. We can decide then."

Merry knew what Caprice meant, but she really didn't want to talk about Shellie Hughes's miraculous revirgination plans. Shellie had once said, "There are two important things to a fortyish woman—a taut throat and a tight twat." This would not be featured on a pillow.

They met at the Royal Palais Café on 57th Street, where the service was quick, the coffee was good, and the check came with the coffee. The clientele resembled a central-casting audition for a "Somebody Who Looks Like Somebody" Convention—the polyester-clad extras who filled the restaurants and streets in the dramas of everyone else's lives; the faces of the has-beens and the never-weres. The waiters, except for their long white long aprons, looked interchangeable with the male customers. The henna-haired cashier lounged behind the register in the pose she no doubt employed with great skill when she was a hat-check girl at one of the midtown nightclubs—fifty years ago. Like exiles from their long-faded planets of youth and promise, the patrons sat nursing their Rob Roys and Manhattans, while the cuisine of egg salad or tuna sandwiches garnished with rapidly wilting lettuce sat untouched on thick white diner-style plates. Lonely men and women sat with vacant stares, as if they were looking at the newsreels of their lives projected on memory screens in their heads. The most expensive item on the menu was the chicken pot pie for $6.95. But no one ordered it, except on Sunday when it included soup and dessert.

Two

Merry and Caprice were led to a booth in the back of the restaurant, where the business crowd ate.

"You really don't know, do you?" Caprice asked as she checked her makeup in the back of the spoon. It was strictly paint-by-numbers, just as the beauty advisor at Bergdorfs had diagrammed on the generic face map given to all clients. From her forehead to her chin, Caprice was a porcelain wonder, a fragile beauty. In college, Carol Ann Preston had had a nose like a bald eagle and skin resembling the craters of the moon. These infirmities caused her to be somewhat promiscuous, and the eventual result was disastrous. She thought she was pregnant.

As angry as both sets of parents were, they agreed that what was done was done and chipped in to buy a one and a half carat diamond engagement ring for Carol Ann and a set of matching wedding bands for the bride and groom. But they were too upset, they all agreed, to have the rings engraved. After a hasty wedding—comprised of the immediate family, which meant both sets of non-smiling parents, in her grandparents' living room, a JP, and no champagne, just cake and punch—Carol Ann and her groom took off on his motorcycle for a weekend honeymoon. That night, Carol Ann got her period, and the poor groom sped off on his vintage three-more-payments motorcycle, hit a deer, and flew over a cliff. After the funeral, Carol Ann returned her engagement and wedding rings to the jewelers and the wedding gifts to the stores. She got refunds on deposits for furniture for the apartment and hung on to the wedding check gift from her grandparents. In all, the unconsummated marriage produced almost $10,000 in cash.

That was more than enough for Carol Ann to transform her less-than-desirable features into a new nose and porcelain skin. The rest of the money allowed her to look for a job in New York. Lucky Carol Ann. On her first interview she was hired by *Destiny Story* magazine to read submissions. Success came easily.

Marriage number two soon followed and was much better. It lasted for two weeks. Then her husband died unexpectedly, or so the tearful widow sobbed. How unfortunate that the guy had neglected to tell his possessive ex-girlfriend that he was getting married. One night, she followed the groom to his newlywed apartment, waited until Carol Ann went out, and clobbered him with one of his twenty-pound weights. He liked to work out. Carol Ann was distraught—until she learned that the insurance policy he had taken out, at the behest of the former girlfriend, made his wife the beneficiary of a $50,000 insurance policy.

There she was, twenty-four years old and twice a widow. Without a pause, Carol Ann undertook a degree in journalism at NYU and after graduation got a job as an assistant editor at *Obsession*, a rapidly growing porn magazine. There, she met Gordon Smart, the art director.

Marriage number three was somewhat better. She was now Caprice. The marriage lasted all of eighteen months, when the love of her life informed her that he was leaving her for a man. The settlement was more than she had expected—$100,000, because he could well afford it, but also because Mr. Ex-husband-to-be realized that he had not only made a terrible mistake in trying to marry but had no doubt ruined a trusting young woman's life.

The stock market was good to Caprice, the bond market even better, and her next job, as an associate editor at the new *Zee Zee* magazine, more than paid the bills. Merry decorated her apartment.

Merry got right to the point. "So what do you think you heard?"

"I think Shellie had some below-the-belt surgery, if you know what I mean."

Merry stirred her coffee. "I hate to disappoint you, but it's hardly news. But she asked me not to say anything."

"Why not? Aren't I a friend?"

"You are, sweetie, but not with secrets."

"But she told you." Caprice sounded hurt.

"Anyone can tell me anything. Who am I going to tell? The waiter?"

Their salads came. More coffee came. The check was left on a small plate.

"Why would she want to do that? Who looks there?" Cappy asked, her electric-blue eyes opened wide in pure innocence. "Wouldn't she be better off getting her eyes done or some lipo? Who doesn't need some lipo?" Caprice asked the question with the gravity of a press correspondent at a national security briefing.

Merry knew better than to continue the conversation. Caprice was still Carol Ann after all. Never had a clue, yet luck found her anyway. But she was good at her job. No one could punch up a story like "Why I Let My Man Cheat on Me with His First Wife and Her Lesbo

Lover." That issue was a sellout, and she was promoted with a sizeable raise. She also earned her one-name status and embarked on her own monthly fashion column, "Porndornment." It was an immediate success. Everyone in the industry was now reading the much-anticipated quips on the best and worst fashions from the "Porndornment" insert, "Thong in Cheek." Plus, she'd come up with a new fragrance called "Thesaurus—The gift to give when words fail you." Dumb luck. Just dumb luck.

"Maybe I should do it. What do you think?" Caprice asked.

"Do what?"

"You know, the thing Shellie's doing." Caprice was again checking her eye makeup, this time using the knife blade as a mirror.

"That depends. You do use it, don't you?" Merry was astounded Caprice was asking her. But she guessed nothing was too personal.

"I wish. I'm sort of out of circulation since Gordon..." Her voice trailed off as if in a reverie. "It's funny, really. So long ago. He runs off with a guy and even takes the condoms. Then, after all these years, I bumped into both of them at Bloomie's last week. They were buying towels. Towels!" Caprice broke into tears. "We never bought towels. We used the ones from when I was with Larry. Gordon didn't mind using a murdered man's towels, but he told me he always felt funny sleeping with a dead man's wife."

"Come on, Cappy, pull yourself together. Your mascara's melting."

"This is supposed to be waterproof. Damn. Thirty-five dollars for nothing. Do I look like a clown?"

The kind reply was, "Oh, Cappy, you could never look like a clown."

Three

No sooner had Merry returned from lunch when the phone service rang with six messages—all urgent. I need those wallpaper samples. When is my muffin stand coming? Should I go completely country French or just accessorize? The drapes are too short. The carpenter put the valences on upside down. The armoire doors squeak. The usual, on and on, with each caller's anxious message sounding as if she were urgently waiting for a heart transplant.

The workday sped by. Then a quick fix-up of the face, and she was off to cross the bridge of time to Randy's apartment.

Randy was *the* Randall Alden Grant—one of those elegant city denizens who actually drank water that came from the kitchen faucet. Unlike some West Siders, who drank Evian and Perrier from jelly jars, Randall Alden Grant sipped city water from a Baccarat crystal tumbler. Everything in his co-op was orderly, polished, elegant, antique, and inherited. His architectural firm, third generation, was internationally known. The firm, with its steady stream of clients, some of whom also were third generation, was inherited as well, as was the wealth of said clients. Randy kept in touch with friends from his MIT days through his annual Christmas card list. Even their children received birthday cards with modest gift certificates from Rizzoli's. These friends were some of his most loyal clients and best referrals. Every year, starting the week after Thanksgiving, Randy held an open house from five to seven on Thursdays for those who were in the city for Christmas shopping. Almost everyone showed up at least once, even if they weren't there for shopping. Caterers loved to do Grant parties, which always were elegant and generous. For Randy, they were a business expense and "so fun."

The sun was setting as Merry headed for Randy's apartment, and the first chill of a late-fall breeze shepherded unruly litter along the sidewalk, pushing it against shop and restaurant doors. No one noticed. To the city dweller, the cacophony of sidewalk drilling, traffic noise, and exhaust melded with the litter and pungent aromas of street vendors' stands of hot pretzels and roasting chestnuts. The crush of humanity was no more noticeable than the beat of one's heart or an eyelash on the cheek.

Merry pulled her mohair scarf closer to her neck. It felt scratchy. As she approached the street opposite Randy's building, she looked up to see the amber lights glowing from the covered terrace of his penthouse co-op. If he ever sold it, the real-estate listing would read "Pk Vue. WBF. EIK. Prewar bldg." Also inherited. Another one with all the luck.

Four

October 1974

Merry and Randy first met in Boston at La Viola's annual autumn open house to view the new lines as well as enjoy the fabulous catered spread, which was in itself a display worthy of the attention of the invited press. The Sunday papers always carried a story about the open house, along with incredible photos. The guest list included old clients and prospective clients, and building-industry scions, hotels owners, restaurant owners, and architects who employed the talents of La Viola.

They introduced themselves, as Randy put it, across the cheese board, in front of the Brie. Randall Alden Grant, architect. Merry Dawn Venture, proudly wearing a badge identifying her as a designer trainee at La Viola of Newberry Street.

Merry was new to Boston, and her small-town New Hampshire wardrobe proclaimed a total lack of city fashion, let alone personal style. Awkward in her high-school wardrobe, Merry stood out at the gathering, almost an anachronism among the well-dressed and well-groomed throng that was engaged in the camaraderie of success and networking, enjoying champagne and the fabulous spread, all while looking at the exotic textiles and furniture they would be ordering for their clients.

There she was, a round-shouldered girl in a flimsy gray cotton dress, accessorized with a beginning-to-crack imitation patent-leather belt and a pair of seen-better-days black flats. With dull mouse-brown hair and pinched features, she hovered at the edge of the buffet table, looking with hungry eyes at the swirl of activity around her, wishing she could be anyplace but where she was. She nearly jumped in fright when one of the guests approached her with a friendly greeting.

"Hello, I'm Randy Grant. Are you with one of the companies?"

Merry was face-to-face with an astonishingly handsome man who looked to be in his mid-twenties. Tall and bronzed, with sun-bleached hair, eyes the color of warm topaz, and an exquisite warm smile that indicated years of orthodontics. For a moment, Merry stood transfixed, at a loss for words.

"No, I work here," she finally said as she twisted the back of her belt while clenching her toes inside her old flats. "I make drawings for Mr. La Viola." Then in a rush of words, she told this stranger how she'd gotten the job through Morneau's Furniture Store in Kerry Lakes, New Hampshire, where she had worked for three years after high school. As she continued her monologue, she twisted her belt too hard, and it snapped. A piece of it plopped onto the large round of apricot-crusted baked Brie. Horrified, she clenched her toes even tighter, and the worn leather on the top of her left shoe popped away from the thin sole.

Randy tried to suppress a laugh, but he couldn't. As Merry's face turned red and she looked as if she were about to faint, he quickly intervened.

"It's warm in here, and you look like you could use some air. Let's go outside for a minute."

He put a protective arm around Merry and started toward the door, while catching the eye of Reno La Viola, Merry's employer. Both men nodded in agreement.

No sooner had Merry and Randy stepped outside than Reno followed them and handed Merry her purse.

"You left this. See you tomorrow."

The kindness in his voice comforted her in her moment of complete embarrassment. Merry gave a meek smile and then stood motionless.

"I'll take you home," Randy said. "Where do you live?" His voice held the same kindness.

"It's okay. I can go alone. It's just down the street at the Standish House for Women." In contrast to the men, her voice sounded like that of a frightened little girl.

"No, no, it's late and too dark. Besides, the walk will do me good."

So, in silence they walked through the deserted area that during the day swarmed with activity.

Ahead, the lights of the Standish House cast a dim illumination onto the deserted street, giving the area a grim and haunted atmosphere. In the dark, the building looked like a warehouse, a repository for the lonely. Merry was among that cadre. Still at a loss for words as they approached the building, she cleared her throat and croaked out, "Thank you for walking me home."

"All in the line of duty."

When they reached the door, she forced out another thank you and a good night, and then scurried into the building like a frightened mouse.

Randy returned to the party, met a stunning Radcliffe grad who represented a leading textile manufacturer, and asked her out for a drink.

The Standish House for Women was a respectable place for young women with no particular future who knew they would be plodding away at low-paying jobs in insurance companies, banks, and retail establishments, with the dim hope that one of the college-grad guys—the insurance or banking trainees in their Brooks Brothers suits— would ask them out. They typed and filed in offices until four thirty every day and then shuffled off to the MTA, the public transportation that, for them, led to nowhere but more of the same tomorrow.

The slender girls with good looks easily got jobs in the Newberry Street dress shops. The ones with looks and brains and secretarial skills worked in art galleries or as receptionists in various real estate, dental, and legal offices Those who had the look of refinement and breeding, so cherished by the upscale retail establishments, found employment with Shreve, Crump & Low and other Valhallas of Back Bay shopping. Those with no skills, fair looks, and nicely manicured hands found themselves parked behind the department-store jewelry counters all over town. Those jobs paid less than the insurance companies and banks, but the girls deluded themselves into thinking they were not part of the thundering herd the Berkeley Street MTA belched up each morning. It was the conceit of the hopeless condescending to the hapless.

Merry got her job because of her experience at Morneau's Furniture Store, her talent, and a portfolio of finely executed sketches that had been born of her imagination and honed by a decorating school correspondence course. She'd been hired at La Viola on her first try. Reno La Viola was an MIT grad in architecture and design and knew talent when he saw it, and he and Mr. Morneau had been roommates at Greyden.

Five

A piece of paper blew up from the street and landed on her scarf, interrupting Merry's reverie. She brushed it away. The doorman greeted her as if she had been there just yesterday. A year had passed, yet he never forgot who went up to see Randall Grant. Randy, Merry knew, was a great tipper.

Faint aromas of expensive perfume, Chinese takeout, and saddle leather lingered like ghosts trapped forever in the carved walnut interior of the elevator. Merry imagined a little girl in 4-D who took riding lessons in Central Park. The kitchen in 6-A had never been used, except to heat up kung pao chicken. Randy had told her that the duplex on eight was inhabited by a woman who went out only to smuggle in bottles of Scotch, apparently fooling no one by anointing herself with gallons of My Sin, the perfume she had delivered.

At the penthouse floor, the polished brass elevator doors opened with stately restraint, revealing a private entrance surrounded by marble and polished mahogany. It was grand— just as it had been when it was built in the mid-1920s, before the stock market crash. Not one hint of disrepair. Not even a crack in the high-domed ceiling.

Merry rang the bell. Randy opened the door, greeting her with the familiarity of an old friend. *How could a year pass but feel as if it were only a day?* It was just a breeze of a thought, wafting past the edges of her mind.

"Well, you look the same," Randy said. "How do you do it, kiddo?" He always called her kiddo when things were going well with them.

Merry immediately wondered what Randy was up to. "I drink a cup of formaldehyde for breakfast. The undertaker delivers it fresh every morning."

"Pasteurized?"

"Ha-ha. Very funny. For your information, it's never pasteurized, but it does come in chocolate flavor. But I prefer it plain. Fewer calories."

"Have a drink?" He handed her a crystal goblet filled with fragrant Spanish sherry. No one could get this rare sherry anymore, but Randy never seemed to run out.

Merry nestled into a deep chair in front of the fireplace and watched the flames dance like graceful sprites in diaphanous gowns of red and orange chiffon. As she sipped her drink, she felt the warm glow of the aromatic beverage lulling her into a sense of comfort. The sherry warmed her chilled heart and etched a softened smile into her face.

"Why the call?" she asked. "I thought I'd dropped off your radar screen."

Randy looked uncomfortable. No answer. A burning log split and fell in the fireplace. The fire sprites hissed with annoyance.

"I suppose I should have kept in contact while I was working in Europe," he finally said. "I had things to think through."

"What things?" *Be casual, Merry,* she told herself. *You might hear something you don't expect. But what if he asks…? Don't be ridiculous. All you asked was, "What things?"*

"Well, we're both getting there, aren't we?" he said.

"Speak for yourself, Randy."

"You really don't know what I'm getting at, do you?"

"No, I don't. Look, it's getting late. I think I'd better go." *You idiot.* Why had she said that? She'd just gotten there. Couldn't she listen for a minute?

Randy, looking down, spoke as if he were in conversation with his wine glass, his voice slow and thoughtful. "Come on, Merry, you just got here. Don't go. I know I was a RPITA."

"What the hell does that mean?" *Why am I so touchy? I wish I could be anywhere but here.*

"A royal pain in the ass." He looked up at her with a twinkle in his eyes and his "come on; don't be mad at me" little-boy grin.

"You were," she said, "but that was a year ago. Time wounds all heels, as the saying goes."

"What I'm getting at is that I'm sorry. Let's not mess up a longtime friendship. I want to be friends. You?"

"No sense in going through life mad. Why not give it a shot?" *That's because of your big mouth, Merry. You ruin things before they ever happen. Just friends.*

"That's my Merry."

Silence again. Not long, just enough for Randy to introduce a new subject.

"I'm getting married. Next summer."

"You invited me here to tell me that? Why couldn't you have just sent me an invitation? What do you want for a wedding present? A toaster?"

"Things happen. I told you I had things to think over."

"So who is she? Anyone I know?"

Merry found it difficult to keep up the sham of glibness. Whatever she had expected to happen at this unexpected reunion with Randy, it certainly didn't include this hit-to-the-solar-plexus surprise. As always, she had nurtured the feeble hope that somehow Randy would see through her guarded actions or would read her unspoken thoughts, as if there were a transparent screen across her forehead that revealed what she hoped for but could not express, or even admit to herself. It was like a child wanting something, yet afraid to ask for it and then being disappointed when others got what she wanted. As far as Randy was concerned, she knew she was a long-term casual friend for whom he had no romantic feelings. Yet she still tormented herself with that immature hope, always lingering on the horizon of her unfulfilled dreamscape.

Randy poked the fire. "I don't think you know her."

"Why the secrecy? Is she in a witness protection program? Or are you waiting for her to get out of high school?" *Keep it light; don't show your feelings. But how do I really feel about Randy? Do I love him? Could I love him? No and no. So why am I so shocked that he found someone? I've never encouraged him, so why should he think…? Keep it light, kiddo, keep it light.*

He looked at her. "My goodness, do I detect a whiff of…? No, it couldn't be. But yes, it is! Eau de Bitchy." His expression changed subtly, as if he were silently asking her, "What did you expect?"

"Wrong, wrong, wrong," she said. "You just surprised me." She took another sip of her sherry, which now tasted like an elixir of disappointment. She finished the last drop and placed the goblet on a small silver tray.

"Still friends?" Randy asked.

"Why not? I'm not the one who had to think things over. Seriously, I am happy for you. We're friends. It's not that we were… but if we were…" Still trying to cover her shock and strange feelings of disillusionment and disbelief, Merry forced a laugh. "I would have included a loaf of bread with the toaster."

Randy did not make a retort this time but placed his own glass on the tray and stood up, signaling the visit was over.

"Good," he said. "Look, I'm really hungry. Let's grab some dinner. I made reservations." He smiled warmly at her.

"Pretty sure of yourself, aren't you?"

"Why do you say that?" And he put his arm around her shoulders in a good-buddy sort of way as they left his apartment.

Six

November 1994

In the days following that evening with Randy, Merry finally became painfully aware of the slow descent of the limbo pole of her self-deluding romantic fantasies. How adroit she had become over the years in concocting a protective shell that grew thicker around her as time went on. Maybe she should have been honest with Randy. But honest about what? That she was frightened of being hurt? Maybe she had been too casual around him.

You guess? she asked herself.

Not once had she shown anything remotely encouraging toward him. All she had been was his pal, his big-mouthed verbal sparring buddy.

The same realization repeated itself with the dullness of walking on a treadmill. Then the cold, damp feeling of loneliness wrapped around her again, creating the sensation of being in the coiled grip of a boa constrictor. There'd been no phone calls from Randy since that quick drink in his apartment and the hastily consumed dinner. No wedding invitation in the mail. No announcement in the papers. Merry, her own expert social surgeon, had excised any hopes for her future.

She did not call Randy. It was that game again. If he didn't call her, she wouldn't call him. But it really wasn't too late to thank him for a pleasant evening. The silence finally got to her, and she called Randy at his Park Avenue office. A receptionist told her he was out of town. No message had been left for her.

Well, that was that. She well knew that limbo poles and treadmills did not have destinations.

Seven

December 1994–January 1995

The weather changed abruptly from a windy late autumn to the chill of a New York winter. A November flurry left a dusting of snow on the edges of shop and restaurant awnings, giving the appearance of dandruff on an old man's lapel. Thanksgiving swept by, and then the Christmas season descended, marked by gifts of imported cheeses and good wine from thankful fabric houses. The smaller accessory houses sent tasteful greeting cards. The more important furniture houses just sent catalogs for the coming year and lists of furniture show dates. Nothing from Randy.

Then it was finally winter, with snow falling into the eyes of rushing pedestrians as an incessant ringing of jingling bells pierced the crisp air. Everyone from somewhere else had converged on the city, crowding the restaurants and jamming the aisles of the department stores.

Like clockwork, Merry's loyal clients either called for appointments or took the chance of dropping by to talk about their plans for spring redecorating before they took off for the warmer climate's social season. "Planning ahead is such a good idea" seemed the mantra of her devotees of duvets. "Do it before everything starts." Parties, dinners, wardrobe fittings, dieting. Merry always served her clients those fancy imported cheeses and wines sent to her by the thankful wholesale houses that hoped for another year of good orders.

The holidays came and passed. Merry spent New Year's Eve in the office. It was a good time to get proposals ready for mailing the following week. New Year's Day, she slept. The phone rang a couple of times, but she didn't hear it. She had turned down the volume until it was almost inaudible. The pillow over her head didn't help.

When Merry finally awoke, it was dark. *Three hundred and sixty-four more days of this,* she mused as she re-adjusted the volume on the phone. The kitchen larder offered instant coffee and a stale Danish, which, since she was feeling sorry for herself, she figured was all she deserved.

You are not very nice to yourself, you know.

Yeah, I know. So just let me dunk the damn Danish and get on with my life.

The too-loud ringing of the telephone shattered the air.

"Hello?"

"Well, where have you been, kiddo?" Randy sounded as if he had found a long-lost sock in the back of a dresser drawer.

"Where have I been? Where have you been? I might ask."

Okay, Merry, here's your chance to start the New Year off with no more games. Just tell him... what? That I wished we could get to the point in our relationship? But what point?

"Okay," he said. "So then where are your manners? A guy takes an old friend out for dinner and no thank-you call?"

"I'll put it on the six o'clock news. I thought you were going to call me. Weren't you concerned that I was abducted on the way home? And by the way, I'm not that old." *Or am I?* Merry wondered.

"I have something I want to show you. Come over in an hour."

"What makes you think I want to see anything of yours?"

"Just shut up and come over."

Eight

April 1964–July 1970
Sad memories, long suppressed, were all she had of her life with her family in Kerry Lakes. Those memories, though now dulled, still bore enough sharp and jagged edges. The only child of Glenda and Doug Venture, Merry was a quiet, awkward girl, prone to retreating into her imagination, fueled by her solitary trips to the local movie house that showed reruns of films from the thirties and forties.

The theater was run as a hobby by a local merchant. Merry frequently was a lone spectator in the quiet auditorium, watching *Mildred Pierce, Jezebel,* and *Kitty Foyle.* Saturdays were a double feature. Sometimes she sat through them twice.

This was her classroom and her finishing school. Merry firmly believed that a ticket to the movies was also a ticket to escaping Glenda, Doug, and Kerry Lakes.

Celluloid images of mansions with iron gates, marble fireplaces, and gilded furniture, inhabited by "nice" people in magnificent clothing, filled the giant screen of the darkened movie house. These impressions were branded like a hot iron on her young mind. This was how it would be some day. This was what her life had to become. But what kind of miracle would have to intervene to cause it all to happen?

At home, Merry would sketch the movie sets, the costumes, the jewelry, even the enormous silver tea services that were lugged around by slipper-footed servants. But it was the way the actors spoke that really intrigued her. If she couldn't live that life, then at least she could sound as if she did. At twelve years of age, Merry Venture of Railroad Street perfected the most self-conscious stage-British accent and overly dramatic oratory that could be paved over a rural New Hampshire twang.

"Yo'ah jest a big phony with that accent. Why cahn't ya jest act nahmal? Such ayhers. Really." Glenda Venture continued beating the mashed potatoes with a vengeance worthy of a loan shark's henchman giving a welsher a twenty-four-hour warning to come up with the cash or else. "If ya ahsk me, yo'ah jest tryin' to make people think yo'ah bettah than they ahr. But they'ah on to ya."

The helpless potatoes yielded to the muscle that Glenda was inflicting on them as the mass became lighter than whipped cream.

"Yoah fahthah is completely disgusted with ya. No wondah he's always so sad. Jest breakin' ahr hahts. Jest breakin' ahr hahts."

"That is a rahther int'resting but quite incorrect observation, muthah, deah." Merry continued setting the small table, which was crammed into the tiny kitchen of their four-room house. "Howevah, I shall improve myself, or I shall always be stuck he'ah in this desolate quagmi-ah of perpetual disappointment and despai-ah called Kerry Lakes. Believe me, I shall strive... Oh, extinguish the anguish of my unfortunate existence!"

Joan Crawford could not have delivered those lines without winning an Academy Award.

"Ha! That's what I thought too. Once. But when yo'ah fahthah ahsked me to marry him, I knew everything would tuhrn out fine."

That wasn't at all true. At just a week shy of his sixteenth birthday, Doug Venture had been forced into a hasty marriage with the not-quite-fifteen-year-old Glenda Armstrong, thus ruining her chance to work in the mill and his chance to learn auto mechanics. There they were, expectant parents after one summer afternoon of mattress Olympics in the back of his father's half-ton pickup. Doug's part-time job at the hardware store became an unwanted career choice, and Glenda worked at the Busy Bee Luncheonette until she couldn't fit behind the counter. They had dug their graves. Time would fill them in.

By the time Merry was fourteen, Glenda was almost thirty, and her youth had long ago been replaced by a prematurely old woman, out of shape, fat, and grumpy. But she always smiled when she slapped the menu down on the counter with a cheery, "What'll it be, dearie?"

Merry finished setting the table. The last part of the nightly ritual was to put out the floral-printed water glasses that had once held pineapple cream cheese.

The conversation stopped. Doug Venture was home from the hardware store. The day was officially over. The three of them sat in gloomy silence, eating the predictable Tuesday night supper: meatloaf, canned peas, and tortured potatoes, followed by a dessert of half a canned pear with a brownie square from the A&P. Merry cleared the table. Glenda washed the dishes. Merry dried. Doug left the house to go bowling. No one said good-bye.

Merry never did homework. She considered attending high school something to be painfully endured. Each morning after she mounted the steps to the drafty yellow-brick building, she ran to the girls' room and got sick. She would stay there until the first period bell rang. Awkward and alone in the school corridors, she passed the popular kids who clumped together in their mutual admiration for one another, not giving a thought to the shy girl who never knew what was going on in class and was always daydreaming. A wall was between them, a wall constructed by young people who defined themselves by good grades and good looks, and certainly did not live anywhere near Railroad Street. Merry often wondered if she smelled bad or had stepped in something. Just to make sure, she would look at her shoe soles.

At fourteen, she got her working papers for a part-time after-school job at Morneau's, the local furniture store whose window banner proudly boasted that every bride who bought a cedar hope chest would receive a free Martha Washington-style bedspread. For Merry, it was a wonderful place to work. The aroma of furniture polish mingled with the new rug smell was her favorite perfume. Every day after school and on Saturdays, she would dust and polish the furniture, all the while pretending that each model room was where she lived. One Saturday, she found some dishes that had been left over from a sales promotion, and she lovingly set the grand mahogany dining table. If she squinted in just the right way, she could obliterate the sign announcing that an extra chair was included as a bonus when matching pieces were purchased.

For her sixteenth birthday, she put her savings into a correspondence course on decorating. She sketched chairs, tables, sofas, and lamps in her classroom note-books. Her talent did not go unnoticed. Impressed by her renderings, Mr. Morneau promised Merry a job when she finished high school.

Merry graduated from high school with a D-plus average, the plus awarded for a poorly executed home economics project. She created a casserole recipe using canned mushroom soup, potato chips, and canned shrimp. Rather than fail Merry for omitting how to cook this obvious mess, the teacher awarded her a half point to keep her out of the class the following year, thus assuring her graduation.

Merry began her new full-time job at Morneau's. She used part of her paycheck for a room at Grace and Carl Pritchard's rooming house. It was a good place for a nice girl to live. Grace Pritchard was the church organist, and Carl taught Sunday school. Merry was comfortable in her little cell of a rented attic room. For graduation, Mrs. Morneau gave her a white Martha Washington bedspread.

Nine

June 1948

Glenda Clara Armstrong was a cute kid—a tomboy and a daredevil. Packed into her sturdy eleven-year-old frame was boundless energy and wild curiosity, held together with good nature and a delicious sense of humor for the profoundly vulgar that appealed only to preadolescent girls and boys. Glenda was also a popular poet during recess. She held center stage, and in a low voice, so the recess monitors couldn't hear, she intoned, with appropriate giggles from her rapt audience:

"Ziggidy Ziggidy Zus.
My muthah don't like me to cuss.
But damn it to hell ah lahk it so well
If ah don't do it ah think ah will bust.
Hell once, hell twice,
Sayin' this is verray nice.
God damn, Ziggity Zam.
That's the kind a person ah am."

Screams of laughter alerted Miss Middleton, the recess monitor, to investigate this unseemly outburst. "And just what is going on here, I might ask?"

The girls shuffled their feet and mumbled, "Nothing."

Miss Middleton put on her famous "old maid witch face" while the girls assumed the most innocent of faces. "Well, whatever you were up to—and I suspect you, Glenda

Armstrong—do not do it again." And off she went just as the bell rang to signal the end of a most enjoyable recess.

One day, as Glenda was trudging off to school (her parents had taken her bicycle away because they'd caught her riding it at breakneck speeds with her eyes closed), she reached into her pocket and removed one of the white balloons she had taken from her father's dresser. *I guess he's plannin' a surprise birthday pahty for muthah,* she mused while she attempted to blow the funny-looking balloon to its biggest size. Later, at recess, with her characteristic generosity, she handed out the white balloons to her friends. All six girls stood in a circle and attempted to blow the balloons up, but the mouthpiece end was too wide. Glenda held hers in her teeth and stretched it out as far as it would go.

Once again, Miss Middleton was the recess monitor, and she saw what that little ringleader was doing. Her face red and her neck veins bulging, she shrieked, "What are you doing with that?"

"My balloon? I'm blowin' it up."

"Go directly to the principal's office. Now."

Harrumphing all the way, Miss Middleton marched ahead of Glenda into the school. Without knocking, she barged into the office of Mr. Edgar Collins Cushing. At that very moment, he was in a most compromising pose with Miss Bowers, the remedial reading teacher. Right there in the supply closet, with the door open.

He shoved Miss Bowers away from him. "Well, Miss Bowers, my sincere condolences to you and your family on the sudden death of your great-aunt Phoebe. Take the rest of the day off and be with your family."

And without missing a beat, the bald, corpulent, beady-eyed Mr. Edgar Collins Cushing turned to Miss Middleton and intoned, with unctuous interest, "Yes, Miss Middleton, what may I do for you and Glenda?"

Glenda was now twisting the balloon around her index finger as Miss Middleton spoke with as much composure as she could muster, considering her shock at what she had just seen. "It seems that Glenda has brought some items to school and has shared them with her friends."

"What are these items, Glenda?" Mr. Cushing could see full well what the little girl was twisting around her fingers.

"Balloons," Glenda said. "White balloons. I found them in my fahthah's nightstand. I think he's plannin' a birthday pahty for my muthah, because he has dozens of them all rolled up like pahty fayvahs."

"I see," said the principal. "Well, just throw it away and go back outside. And you know you should not be rummaging around in places that are not yours. Go along."

Glenda dumped the balloon into the wastebasket and skipped out to her friends, who told her once again that the balloons were awful because the mouthpieces were too wide to blow in.

"Miss Middleton," Mr. Cushing said to her, "you look as if you are going to faint. Perhaps a sip of medicinal brandy?"

"Thank you, no. I do not indulge—I mean, imbibe. Water. I need water." She grasped her scrawny neck as she sucked in her cheeks in righteous indignation. What infuriated this paragon of spinsterhood was that two years ago, Mr. Cushing had made—or so she had thought—an unwanted advance on her person during a salary conference. What the poor soul hadn't realized was that a huge spider was dropping from the ceiling and was about to land on her all-but-nonexistent bosom.

Mr. Cushing's quick, innocent action of trying to sweep away the potentially offensive arachnid so frightened the poor woman, she nearly swooned. When he explained the perceived offense, she claimed to have forgiven him. But Miss Middleton certainly would not forget.

Mr. Cushing handed her a paper cup filled with water from the office cooler. "Miss Middleton, I've been thinking about you for some time, and I want to commend you on your performance as a teacher. A very valuable teacher in our big family of teachers. Dedicated and loyal teachers are rare—very rare—and you, Miss Middleton, are among the rarest. I think a little bonus will be coming your way before the Christmas vacation. You'd like that, wouldn't you?"

Miss Charlotte Emily Middleton put on her most professional teacher face, and with her characteristically pursed lips, managed to intone, "Yes, thank you. Thank you so much. Yes, thank you."

"Then it will be our little secret." Mr. Cushing cleared his throat. "We don't want the others to know, but you certainly deserve a bonus. Now, let's get on with the day."

"Little bonus, indeed," Miss Middleton muttered to herself as she strode out of the principal's office and headed for her classroom.

As soon as he was alone, Mr. Cushing went directly to the supply closet and removed the box of white balloons stashed behind the paper clips and the pile of hymn books donated by the local insurance company. After locking them in his desk, he sat down and lit a cigar.

Three years later, Glenda would learn the real use for the balloons. She knew to always use one the second time. The first time didn't count, because you didn't know if you'd like it. At least, that's what her friends said. But Glenda was the first of her friends to find out—and the only one who left school in the middle of her freshman year.

Ten

January 1995

An icy rain was falling when Merry left her apartment. Walking even the short distance to Randy's was impossible, as a layer of ice covered the streets. By the time she finally got a cab, the rain had turned to small pellets of hail. Even though it was late on New Year's Day, the traffic was impossible. It took twenty minutes to get to Randy's. Wet and freezing, Merry passed by the doorman, shuddered her "good evening," and ascended in the quiet elevator to Randy's sanctuary. The door was open in anticipation of her arrival.

"Cheers," Randy said. "Have a brandy." Merry, still wearing her frozen coat, accepted the proffered drink. "Take off your coat. You are going to stay for a while?"

Randy looked like a magazine ad for the very best of everything: cashmere sweater, silk and wool slacks, not to mention the handmade leather slippers, a symphony in soft beige, with just a hint of pale blue in the cuffs and collar of his shirt.

"Cheers to you too. What's up? Why did you ask me over?"

"A bit of news. I want you to be the first to know because it involves you." Randy put another log on the fire and poked at the embers. A crackling sound broke out in the hearth, while the aroma of fragrant wood floated around the room.

"How am I involved?" Merry's heart was beating too fast and her hands felt clammy. *Maybe he's going to say something about us. What if he does?*

"I'd like to be your client," he said. "I'm building a house. Something both for long weekend getaways and to spend a couple of months in the winter. Interested?" The heat from the fireplace gave his face a bright glow, and his eyes sparkled as he spoke.

Merry did not have a glib retort. This was serious. In all the years she had been in New York, not once had Randy purchased as much as a pillow from her, let alone asked her for decorating advice.

"Why me? I thought you did only English antiques."

"This is something different. As you know, I'm getting married this summer. The house is almost complete. It's in Palm Beach, and I want you to create the La Viola look in it. I need it done in six months. I've already spoken with Reno, and he agrees that you are the one to do it. Say you'll do it."

He made the offer sound adorable... and without consulting her first. He reached for an envelope and removed what looked like a contract and handed it to her.

"What's the matter with your intended?" she asked. "Doesn't she know the difference between a chair and a bed?" Upon taking the sheaf of papers, Merry realized that her repartee was not appreciated and was even being ignored.

Randy's voice no longer had that familiar good-buddy sound but had taken on the distinct tone of a business transaction. "She's not here. She's in England and won't be here until the house is finished and furnished. That's where you come in."

"What style? What colors? No one wants to live in a place they've never seen."

"She and I have already talked about it. You're the one we want to give the place the La Viola touch, and you will be well paid. Take a look at the contract. It's all there."

"Really, why isn't this mystery fiancée involved?"

"Simple. This will be her first house in America. You'll know how to make it look like the perfect weekend and winter getaway. Elizabeth has always lived at her family estate. It's been furnished for generations."

"Oh, so you want it to look American and Palm Beach." Merry's eyes felt watery. "I must be coming down with a cold," she muttered, brushing away what was clearly a tear.

"Could be." Randy ignored her distress—or didn't even notice it.

Merry pulled herself together. "What does the house look like? Where are the plans? I could work from that."

"Better still, why not go down and see it? I'll book a flight for you."

So this was no joke. Randy would be her client. She would work for Randy. This was strictly a business relationship. Suddenly, Merry felt old. "I'm sure I can arrange it. I'll let you know tomorrow morning."

"Fine. Then I want you to come to the office so we can go over the contract, the house plans. I'll explain the rest then. Reno has approved the project, and now we're waiting for you."

That was something Merry liked about Randy. He was always so sure of himself, always so in charge. What was Elizabeth like? But this was not the time to ask her age or, in fact, anything about her. It was Merry who was the "she," the decorator with a to-be-signed contract.

"Look at the time," she said. "I really should get a cab and go home. Big job tomorrow."

"I'll see you to a cab." Randy took an umbrella from the closet and handed it to her. "Bring it to the office tomorrow when you come to sign the contract."

"Yes. Tomorrow."

A new sensation wracked Merry both in body and soul as she felt herself crumbling under the weight of sadness. Her secret inner child at last heard the thud as the limbo pole hit the ground. Her long-imagined dance was over.

In silence, they entered the elevator. And in silence, they stood as Randy hailed a cab. The cold rain mingled with Merry's hot tears as she climbed into the taxi and headed off into the eerie silence of now near-empty streets.

Eleven

January 1995

Weary from the events of the day and chilled by the sleet and rain, Merry entered the small lobby of her apartment building. The night doorman looked up from his newspaper and handed her a package the size of a shoebox. The postage revealed it was from Las Vegas. She didn't know anyone in Las Vegas. The package was well wrapped in heavy brown shipping paper. She shook it. Not a clue.

Once in her apartment, she threw her coat on a chair and shook the box again. With great curiosity, she ripped off the outer wrapping. Still no clue. Taped to the gift-wrapped box inside was a white envelope. "Read this first" was inscribed in a flourish that could only be from the hand of Caprice.

> Dear Merry,
>
> I'm here in Las Vegas on my honeymoon! Can you believe it? It happened so fast. Ty Bascomb, the photo editor, and I are on a *Zee Zee* assignment, and we did it! At an Elvis chapel!!! Surprised? Ty may not be a centerfold glamour boy, but he was single. He's straight and six feet tall. He's also half-owner of *Zee Zee*. Let's hope this one

is for keeps. I sure don't want to end up marrying the director of circulation next.

On second thought, it really didn't happen all that fast. We've been on assignment together for the past two months, and we really work well together. And in more than one way. Guess what he's giving me for a wedding present? Monogrammed towels!!! I really got a bang out of that. So did he.

When we got to the Elvis chapel, Ty handed me my wedding bouquet. I couldn't stop laughing. Anyway, you know I would have had you as my maid of honor if there had been time to really plan this thing. So I'm sending you the bouquet. Don't laugh.

We'll be back when the assignment is over. I'll call you then.

Love,
Caprice (Mrs. Tyler Bascomb)

Merry tore away the gift wrapping and opened the cover of the white satin box. Out sprang a coiled, brilliantly gold rubber phallus the size of a loaf of French bread. The tag read "Bone Appétit." The plastic bag that protected it bore the warning that the bag was not a toy and should not be given to children. The admonishment also stated that the bag should not be used as a head or face covering. Merry doubled up in a convulsion of laughter. This was the funniest gift ever. One thing about Caprice—she knew how to take chances. To make things work and not take herself too seriously. And she had dead aim for her ambitions.

Merry's laughter was cut short when the phone rang. She was surprised to hear Gloria's voice. She tried to choke back her laughter as she held the phone in one hand and clutched the golden phallus in the other.

"Are you choking on something?" Gloria asked.

"No." Merry was still laughing. "So how are you? I haven't heard from you since we all had dinner at Le Cirque. What was it? Three months ago?"

"Just about. I know I should have called, but I was out of the country with my handbag business, and then... Oh, God. What a mess with the divorce."

"You mean that thing is still dragging on?" Merry shook the golden prize, and its springs caused it to quiver.

"What's so funny? My divorce or some other joke?"

"No, Gloria. I'll tell you later, after you tell me what's going on."

"My personal life is still on the crazy side."

"So tell me." Merry propped her pillow up against the headboard of her bed and made herself comfortable.

"I spent last night in Connecticut, a very awful New Year's Eve with my future ex's in-laws. It seems they need reassurance that I'm not going to sue their darling boy for half of his earnings. I asked them if they knew that half of nothing is nothing. Can you believe we've been separated for three years, and all that has to be done is for him to sign the papers?"

"So what's the holdup?"

"He thinks that he earned half of what we own by staying home to write the great American novel while I was out working to support the bum."

"But you already knew that."

"I thought I knew. I really thought he was dragging his feet on signing because he never follows up on anything. Was I surprised when I got a call from my future ex-moth-er-in-law to make my appearance at the old family home on the afternoon of New Year's Eve. The guy's forty-five years old, and he still can't think for himself."

"Couldn't you have done this through your lawyers?"

"I could have. I wanted to. But sonny boy returned to live in the bosom of his family and actually condescended to take a job with Daddy's firm."

"What's he going to do? Go back to practicing law?"

"That moron? I pity anyone using him as counsel. Anyway, his folks are absolutely paranoid that I'm going to go after half of the law firm. I finally convinced them that all I want—and have wanted for the past three years—is out."

"So what's going to happen now?"

"After I thought I had assured them, they insisted I sign away any claim I might have, now or in the future. I told them I'd gladly do so in blood. But he had to agree too, freeing me of any obligation to him. You should have seen their faces. I signed it and took my leave. I have to wait for my lawyer to send the papers to him. It will have to be on lined paper so he can sign it with a crayon."

"You are angry, aren't you?"

"No, just bitter about throwing away three good years when I could have created my own misery without any help from Mister 'I'm writing the great American novel, so do you have any paper?'" Gloria's voice was harsh with the acid of sadness from the lost years and frustration with herself.

"You're worse than bitter," Merry said, "but it's almost over. Guess what? Caprice got married again."

Gloria laughed. "What did she pick this time, a dwarf? A hermaphrodite?"

"This time it isn't a what but a real who. It seems that our little Cappy really landed the big one. He's part owner of *Zee Zee*. Caprice and her dumb luck." Merry was laughing too. "But I'm beginning to think that it's not only luck. Nothing really defeats our girl."

"Yeah," Gloria replied. "Oh, well, tomorrow, I can go back to designing my handbags. I'm calling my new spring line Glad Sacques. The promo will read, 'Don't be a sad sack and carry a grudge when you can tote your stuff in a Glad Sacque, available in Revenge Red, Envy Me Green, Break Up Black, and Don't Pity Me Purple.' Can you believe it? I'm finally able to make the move to Paris. The new line is going to be featured in the Paris Bon Marché, at Harrods in London, and in the Neiman Marcus Christmas catalog."

After promises to get together soon, the two women hung up. Merry waved the giant phallus in the air, musing that Gloria hadn't asked what was going on in Merry's life. But maybe she was just being polite. After all, everyone knew nothing ever happened to Merry, so why ask?

Gloria was the only child of an only child of an only child. Her grandmother and mother had married into large, boisterous, and well-to-do families. As close as Gloria was to her mother, she had learned from her grandmother how to be independent, to take chances, and to follow her heart. Gloria's father was the consummate daddy: loving, generous, and always there to listen. It was a happy family with lots of love and lots of ambition.

It was a cozy life for Gloria Allen; disappointment had not visited her. At thirty-five, she met Clayton Forrest. It was love at first sight, and seemingly of the same mind, they agreed to put marriage on hold until their careers were more firmly established—a euphemism for cold feet. The courtship dragged on for two years while each of them toiled to ensure their professional footholds.

Clay worked in his family's law firm. It was expected of him but not what he wanted. On their honeymoon, he told Gloria that he planned to give up his practice and become a writer. "This is something I have always wanted to do, and I want to do it before it's too late." Gloria was stunned. Her handbag designs were just starting to get significant recognition, and supporting a husband was not what she had in mind. But Clay made it sound all so easy. "I've got money from my trust, and I've saved quite a bit over the years, so we'll be in good shape. Not to worry; everything will be fine."

For the next three years, things weren't fine. Buyers from Paris and London discovered Gloria's design firm, and her business grew by leaps and bounds. She commuted abroad every other month, leaving Clay at home to anguish over his novel. Slowly, they both realized they had made a mistake. They had grown apart. Gloria was now a successful international handbag designer, and Clay had transformed from a man with a purpose to a man with a million excuses for why he couldn't write.

"Did you ever think," Gloria asked him, "that the only block is your head? You had a great future with the firm. You should have stayed with it."

"It's easy for you to say that, but I know I can write this book. Right now, though, something's stopping me. I can't put my finger on it, but something is missing from my life."

"Maybe it's a job. Why couldn't you have stayed with the firm and done your writing on the weekends?"

"Writing is a full-time job. Look, if we're going to have a fight, I'm going out."

"Before you go, pack a suitcase, because you're going to need it."

"So that's what you want?"

"Do I have a choice? All I see is a man going down the drain, taking his opportunities with him."

"What you're telling me is, 'That's it.'"

"Come on, Clay, why do we need to go over this? We both want different things from our lives and our marriage."

"And just what are those different things?"

"Weren't you listening to me? I don't want to go over this again. You know I think you should go back to work. You'd feel better, not so empty."

"I don't need you to psychoanalyze me. But just be sure you want to end this, because once I leave, I'm gone."

"Then consider yourself gone."

"You can send my things to Connecticut."

"You're a big boy. Pack them yourself."

Within an hour, Clay had scooped his belongings into a trunk and three large suitcases. "I'll send someone to pick these up tomorrow," he said, and then he *was* gone.

Gloria plopped down on the sofa and took a deep breath. It finally dawned on her why, for the past year, she had always felt as if she were gasping for air. Now it was time to call her lawyer, sell her apartment, and move on. She announced to the silent living room, "Gloria's finally moving to Paris!" With a sigh of relief, she poured her best merlot into a goblet. She raised her glass in a toast. "To Gloria!"

Twelve

January 1995

Merry sat up in her bed, thinking about what had transpired during this first evening of the new year. She still felt the cold chill of the sleet and rain that drenched her when she left Randy's apartment. That brief meeting with Randy forever changed their association from one of old friends to a formal business relationship. He finalized their status with a contract, giving Merry six months to decorate the house—the one he was building for someone else.

By the time she arrived at her office the next day, she'd already had four phone calls. The only one she chose to answer was the one from Randy's secretary about the time to come by to sign the contract. She called back, arranging to be there within the hour. Now she would call Reno.

"Dear heart, how are you?"

"I'm fine. Better than fine. That's why I'm calling you."

"This sounds interesting. It's not a love thing, is it?"

"No, it's about the big contract for us in Palm Beach, Florida."

"I worked it out with Randy last week, and I know where Palm Beach is. I hope you're excited about this. It's a big opportunity for you."

"The thing is that my—our—new client wants me to go down there to oversee all the decorations. So I'll have to stay there for four to six months. What should I do?"

"That's fine. I know about that too, and it's going to work out well for both of us. I was thinking about having you come back to Boston to help me, but with you going to Palm Beach, this will give you experience with a new market I want to explore. And it will give me the opportunity to send Charles and Edward to Manhattan while you're gone. I'm changing the Madison Avenue image. So I want you to think about coming back to Boston after you finish in Palm Beach. It's a great opportunity for you, and you'd be in the right spot when I retire."

"You're retiring?"

"Not right now, but I need to get all my ducks lined up."

"I'm flattered that you're thinking of me."

"Believe me, this has nothing to do with flattery. You're talented, and you know the business. While you're out of town, how about letting the Gold Dust Twins stay in your apartment?"

"Sure, why not?"

"Call me before you leave so I can arrange things with the new team."

"You got it. And by the way, I think I'd like to be back in Boston again. I'm beginning to feel like I've done the New York thing."

"Haven't met anyone?"

"Not a soul."

"And whose fault is that?"

"Haven't a clue. Bye, Reno, and thanks again."

Thirteen

May 1935–June 1967

For all the years that Merry worked for Reno La Viola, she knew little about him. It was obvious he was very successful, good to work for, and was enormously popular in Boston society with the major donors to the arts who dominated the symphony, museums, and other cultural events. His photograph often appeared whenever major social events were reported in the newspapers. Equally well known on the summer circuit, Reno also was one of the season's elite in Hyannis, Martha's Vineyard, and Nantucket. But in Boston he preferred to be known simply as Reno of La Viola.

For those who remembered, the decorating establishment of La Viola had a long and prosperous history, not only as a thriving business but also for its philanthropy. Giving back to the community was a cornerstone of the company's philosophy.

In the summer of 1935, a young and talented immigrant came to Boston to seek his fortune. Equipped with a sewing machine and a flair for making exquisite draperies, jabots, and festoons, he could work quickly and cheaply from his basement shop on Newberry Street. The nation was in the midst of the Great Depression, but there was in Boston a strata of those who continued to lead a lavish albeit somewhat subdued lifestyle. Within four years, the name of Ruben Laban Volinsky was known by those who demanded perfection at a good price. Ruben lived frugally and soon had a sizable amount of money put aside. Still single at thirty-two, he began to invest his profits in property all over Boston, ultimately amassing blocks of what would become prime real estate. This success could not be ignored by other successful businessmen, some of whom were burdened by daughters well past the age of twenty-five.

It was Calvin Baker who first approached the tall, handsome, gray-eyed man with a suggestion that was worth not only consideration but investigation. Would Ruben consider going into a partnership, investing in the building where Ruben's basement establishment was currently located? Calvin would put up the necessary cash, and Ruben would use his growing business as his share. At the end of a five-year contract, they would share the profits, fifty-fifty. But Calvin suggested more.

Ruben's shop would need to relocate to one of the first-floor retail spaces with a window, where displays could attract more walk-in traffic. That made sense to Ruben, and he warmed to the opportunity to enlarge his growing business. It would require, though, that he take on additional help. That, Calvin Baker said, would not be a problem, as his eldest daughter Bella was an excellent seamstress who happened to be single. Perhaps Ruben might like to meet Bella.

Ah, thought Ruben, *there is always a catch.*

Just by coincidence, as Calvin Baker continued, Bella was passing by outside on the street. Should he invite her to come into the shop? *Not only a catch*, Ruben thought, *but a trap.* With reluctance, he agreed to meet Calvin's daughter. It was love at first sight when he saw Bella, a tall, astonishing, raven-haired beauty, with skin as pale as a white rose and eyes as dark as a midnight sky.

Within three months they were wed. One year later, a son was born.

Now this was a blessing; within the space of just over one year, Calvin Baker's eldest daughter was married, and she produced a son. In the meantime, Calvin focused on a new name for Ruben's shop. It should be something elegant, something European. After all, Calvin Baker, né Chiam Bernstein, knew full well the advantages of a good business name.

One evening he gave serious thought to this metamorphosis. After writing down the name Ruben Laban Volinsky, he rearranged the letters and quickly settled on Reno La Viola. Yes, that was to be the new name for the business, his son-in-law, and his grandson. Now if only he could marry off his other two daughters…

Young Reno was a much loved but hardly spoiled child. Bella set the tone for the disbursements of the growing family fortunes. Ignoring her husband's constant offers of jewels and baubles, she requested—and always gently, for that was her way—that they give to civic charities, where the money would be put to better use than on her fingers, wrists, and earlobes. Ruben, for that was what Bella called him in the house, asked her what he might give her as a personal gift, as he longed to show his love in that way too.

Bella realized this gift meant far more to Ruben; it was part of his male pride. So she requested a rope of pearls, which she would be happy to wear every day for the rest of her life.

As the years passed, the business thrived, the investments prospered, and young Reno was ready for boarding school at Greyden, which was located not far from their home. Reno was well liked by his teachers and a great friend to all, having learned to respect his elders and be fair with his companions. It was Ruben who taught his son that people might like someone because they thought he had money, but once the money was gone, all that person had was his character… and that was gold that could not be hoarded but must be earned daily.

Bella added that Reno should always keep in mind that there were others who did not enjoy the kind of life he did, so he should keep his private life to himself and live his social life with modesty and charity. When he went out with friends, he should wait to see who ordered the least-expensive item on the menu and order the same.

His school years at Greyden brought Reno many friends, especially Billy Morneau of New Hampshire, whose father owned furniture manufacturing factories in the Carolinas and a furniture store in Kerry Lakes. Reno and Billy often talked about their families' mutual credos of giving to charity and looking out for the less fortunate. Best friends often exchange secrets, and Billy told Reno that his grandfather's name was Benjamin Morgenstern. Reno told Billy his father's real name was Ruben Laban Volinsky. When the families met at a parents' weekend, a lifelong friendship was born, and mutual business opportunities blossomed.

In their junior year, Reno and Billy discovered, through casual gossip, that one of the boys in their class, a big spender and a loudmouth, had to leave because his father could no longer pay the tuition.

The once brash and careless Amory Grafton became a withdrawn shadow of his former bravado-clad self. It was rumored that he might kill himself. Some said it was, after all, just a rumor, but Reno and Billy thought otherwise, and they contacted their parents to see what might be done for the distraught Amory.

The next day, as soon as the dean let Amory know that his tuition was paid up for the two final years, he was back to his former antics. Not once did Reno or Billy ever hint at their parents' charity. Both boys agreed that looking for thanks or gratitude was impossible, like trying to sit on a cloud.

His Greyden years behind him, with diligence and enthusiasm Reno earned a degree in architecture from MIT and then entered the family business. With characteristic generosity, his parents established a significant music scholarship fund for underprivileged children. It was his graduation present.

Fourteen

January 1995

The display of glass, marble, polished exotic woods, and good taste at the offices of Randy's firm created a sense of both trust and serenity. A spray of green cymbidium orchids in a Baccarat vase stood on the receptionist's desk. There was not one magazine in the reception area. Randy's philosophy was, if you want to read magazines, go to a library. The focus was on getting to the point. Getting the contract. Getting things done. The philosophy was three generations old. It worked.

Merry had no sooner parked herself in one of the comfortable chairs than Randy strode out of his office to greet her.

"Glad you could make it. Come on in."

Not one pleasantry. And it certainly was not the time for one of Merry's glib remarks.

Architectural drawings covered a large worktable. Next to them was a small stack of papers that looked like a contract. Randy motioned for Merry to sit down.

"These are the house plans. You can look them over later. We don't plan to change anything, so the furniture placement and window treatments shouldn't create any problems. You'll select the bathroom and kitchen electrical fixtures as well as the tiles." As he spoke, Randy rolled up the plans and handed them to Merry. She took them and said nothing.

"The contract is through La Viola with a flat fee for six months of your services, and you can take your usual percentage of the furnishing sales. I'll pay the firm's contractual bonus for each week that you come in ahead of schedule. And don't skimp on anything. This is to be a showplace for Elizabeth. Any questions?"

Merry was speechless at first. Randy, the good-natured pal, was now her employer. "I'll get started this afternoon," she finally said.

"Good. Plan to leave on Friday. On your way out, Sally will give you your round-trip tickets. You'll stay at the Palm Crest Inn. They'll set you up with an office suite. You got everything straight?"

"Yes." Merry offered a weak smile. "Everything's straight."

"Good. I'll be in England for the rest of the month. If you need anything, call the office." This was said as Randy ushered Merry out of his office, leaving her to walk through the reception area by herself.

The meeting had taken no more than twenty minutes, and Merry was out on the street and hailing a cab back to work. The morning was sharp and cold, but the thought of going to a place she had read about so often in trade journals, depicting Florida style, warmed her heart.

Fifteen

November 1983

Shellie, Cappy, and Gloria were all clients of Merry, and all enjoyed great professional and financial success. Of the four, Shellie Hughes was by far the most successful. At twenty-eight, she had been elected a Fellow of the Society of Actuaries. By thirty-two, she was a highly regarded expert in life annuities, and at thirty-seven, a full partner at Parker Sloan McKutchen.

Shellie was not one to leave things to chance. Strategy was everything. At sixteen, she had taken an inventory of her assets. Math: strong. Science: good. Chest: flat. Behind: big. She decided to keep a journal of what needed to be done and how she planned to do it. The math thing would be her meal ticket, but with her looks, she reasoned, there would not be much dessert. The looks were not something she could do much about, at least for now. The guys never bothered with her, except to have her explain math during lunch period in the cafeteria. As soon as lunch was over, they took off like a migrating herd of rutting bison. "If only I could stuff my brains into my bra," she used to say. What a science project that would be! Engineered popularity. The first page in her journal was titled "Scholarship Plans and College Choices." Page two: "Beautification Plans." Page three: "Timetable." The list on each page was numbered one to five. Anything more than that was a waste of time.

The Matt and Betty Hughes family consisted of four bright children—three boys and a girl. The girl was baby Shellie, born years after Frank, Tom, and Mitch, who were already seven, nine, and eleven years old at the time of the unplanned event. The unexpected pregnancy went as trouble free as the other three. The Hughes's never-fail formula had been "Do it, brew it, and a boy will come through it." The thrill of turning out a little girl was more than all five Hugheses could ever have hoped for. The little bundle of joy was the most loved, hugged, and pampered baby daughter and sister in the world.

By the time Shellie was five, she had taught herself to read, as had her brothers. In the first grade, she surpassed her classmates and was transferred to the second grade. The next few years were perfect. Good grades. Fun and friends. Sports. Summer camp. Piano lessons. She took two years of tap and baton but considered them a waste of time. She quit after her tenth birthday. Chess was more fun.

Then one day, Shellie discovered she was no longer a gangly little girl. At five feet seven inches tall, she towered over her seventh-grade classmates, but she never slouched. That is, not until her first year in high school, when she became aware that she was as flat as an ironing board. Almost overnight, the once-confident teenager adopted a round-shouldered stance rivaled only by Quasimodo. The ever-thoughtful Betty came to the rescue with a discreetly padded bra. Confidence restored, Shellie stood up straight and headed for the honor roll. Betty had told Shellie, "Only a boob obsesses over boobs." She loved to make up slogans and mottos.

In her junior year, Shellie realized that all the padding in the world was not going to make up for her anatomical deficit. She was secretary of the math club, having lost her bid for the presidency by two bra sizes.

In the fall of her senior year, her honors math teacher suggested she might want to get an after-school job in the actuarial department at Global Life Insurance Company. Miss Mallory knew of an opportunity for a bright student like Shellie and would be happy to arrange for an interview. Shellie's parents enthusiastically supported her. Shellie added another page to her journal—"Pathways to Success: Stage One."

All but one of the topic headings in Shellie's journal were now complete. After graduating from NYU, she landed her first full-time job at Madison Life Insurance Company in New York. It was a great place to work, and she took advantage of the actuarial training the company provided. After two years, she had saved enough money to finance the second phase of her beautification plan. The first had been interior decoration—her education. The second phase was exterior renovation, which commenced with the long-anticipated boob job to a full 32B. Pointy, delicate. As the French saying went, "Just big enough to fill a champagne coupe," and in American parlance, "A handful." A month later, one of the other actuarial trainees—the one with a jaw like Superman— invited Shellie for a drink after work.

For her twenty-sixth birthday, she gave herself another present she had always wanted. When she told her mother what she was planning to do, all Betty Hughes could do was laugh.

"Mom, I wish I didn't have a BFA."

"You don't have a BFA. Your degree is in math."

"I'm referring to my big, fat ass. I want to have liposuction and get rid of it."

Betty couldn't stop laughing. "What? Slice off the family trademark? When, where, and who is going to do it?"

"I'm researching some specialists in New York. Why? Do you know of anyone?"

Jokingly, Betty responded through her laughter, "How about Dr. Rumpert Slycer? Affectionately known as Rump to his friends."

Then Betty got up, went to the kitchen, and returned with two glasses of wine. The two women sat quietly for a moment, enjoying the first sips of their favorite Napa Valley merlot. "Seriously," Betty said, "if this is what you want to do, then your father and I would like to pay for the surgery. Don't say no. It's your birthday present."

"But I'm making good money, and I saved for this. Really, it's not a problem."

"Then how about our treating you to a nice recuperation vacation?"

"If I say yes, will you promise not to give me any more things?"

"Are you planning to slice off anything else?"

"You'll be the last to know."

They both laughed.

Everything was planned to take place over Shellie's two-week summer vacation, and she had sick days she could use as well. She managed to convince her parents to spend two weeks with her in Bermuda.

When the deed was done and the two-week Bermuda vacation over, Shellie returned to her office looking like a model. Tall and slim, and her hair, once mouse-brown, was now a russet-hued halo—the result of color, highlights, and three day's salary. The transformation was startling.

But Shellie still was the same practical girl she had always been. The next thing on her list was to get that big job, the one that would offer her both financial security and recognition. Within three months, she had lined up an interview at Parker Sloan McKutchen. She came armed with excellent references and was offered a job at a salary that almost made her choke.

"Swallowed the wrong way," she croaked. She did not fool the interviewer. The same thing had happened to him five years earlier.

It was now time to move out of her small apartment in Brooklyn and get a place of her own. Saving money was smart. Investing it was smarter.

By the time Shellie was thirty, her investments in her education, her appearance, and her career were paying off as planned. She found her ideal apartment on Sutton Place. Nice view, big foyer, fireplace in the living room, a window in the kitchen, a big bedroom loaded with closets, and a dressing room and bath.

On October 1, Shellie moved in with a new mattress and a telephone. Her new job at PSK started the next morning. She had a pizza delivered for her dinner. It was the best meal ever. She had almost completed the goals in her journal.

The new job did not change Shellie's work habits or her social life. Everyone at PSK had the same driving work ethic—a tower of drones working from eight to eight.

The first Saturday that Shellie had free, she wandered over to Second Avenue in search of apartment furnishings. On one side of the street, storefront windows featured highly buffed and polished estate furniture—the kind of stuff smart New Englanders auctioned from their dusty barns to New York decorators, who returned like prospectors each summer to cart these castoffs back to the city. There, eager buyers snatched these finds for their apartments. On the other side of the street, window displays featured red patent-leather sofas shaped like lips, chairs crafted like upturned hands, and crouching brass eunuchs holding glass tabletops. The old stuff reminded Shellie of her grandmother's front parlor, but she easily passed on the red lips and upturned palms. She thought she might go home the next weekend and see if there was any stuff in her parents' attic.

A window sign caught her attention: La Viola Interiors. She walked across the street to look in the window. She had found her place.

A slight scent of cinnamon and vanilla lingered in the air of the small yet inviting shop. Tasseled and fringed throw pillows were piled into enormous grapevine baskets. Bolts of bright fabrics with colors as delicious as sherbet lined one of the walls. Black and white toile fabrics covered boudoir chairs clustered around a graceful country-French wood table. Headboards, dressing tables, and loveseats were scattered around the shop in such a way that when a prospective client came upon them, she felt as if she had just made some great discovery. All of the furnishings begged to be taken home. Which ones should she pick? Shellie hadn't a clue.

From the back of the shop emerged a woman about Shellie's age. She greeted her with the warm professionalism that translated into retail-speak as, "Cash, charge, or just looking?" But she had a nice way about her, and Shellie felt at ease.

"I just moved into my apartment, and I don't know what to do with it."

"Then you came to the right place. We can get everything you need."

"I guess I need everything. All I have is a new mattress."

"Why not finish up the bedroom and then work on the rest? How many rooms are there?"

"Only three, but the place is pretty large."

"Three large rooms. I think we can fix it up, but first, you have to tell me what you like. We need to set up an appointment for me to see your place, and after that, I'll give you a preliminary sketch. If it's a go, then we'll discuss fees and your budget for the project."

"Sounds good to me. When can I have an appointment?"

Merry opened the appointment book on the table. "Daytime or evening?"

"Evenings would be better. Eight o'clock?"

"You got it. Next Tuesday?"

The date decided, Shellie gave Merry her address and phone number. Merry gave Shellie her card.

On the way home, Shellie bought a coffee maker and a package of Styrofoam cups. The good stuff was yet to come.

Sixteen

January 1995

With a great sense of relief, Merry packed up her life as she knew it and headed for something new, but it was not with any excitement or anticipation. The past two interactions with Randy had formed her new persona, which would no longer indulge in the persistent *what ifs* of a lonely, unfulfilled life. Now it was her work— and work only. Merry called her clients to let them know she was temporarily transferring to Florida, and that the La Viola team of Charles and Edward would be taking over the Madison Avenue establishment.

Her plane landed at Palm Beach International Airport on time. The parade of deplaning passengers formed a microcosm of winter life in southern Florida.

Women on their annual two-week winter vacations were laden with ten-karat gold necklaces dotted with dull diamond chips. Their fingers, with long red acrylic nails, were adorned with the kind of genuine gemstone rings that appeared in Sunday newspaper ads offering two-day gem-and-pearl sales at the local department store.

Some of the men looked like living testimonials for hair-replacement clubs, fooling no one, as nonmatching wiry gray chest hairs sprouted above the necks of their

T-shirts. Gold chains with anchors, initials, or lion's heads rested between the folds of their not-too-closely-shaven necks. Their annual sojourn in the sunshine.

In the crowd were a few cool blondes who summered in the Hamptons. Pale linen slacks, linen shirts, and pastel cashmere sweaters casually draped over their shoulders identified them as members of the gated golf community crowd. Their discreet jewelry consisted of a pair of small gold earrings, an understated platinum engagement ring set with a flawless sapphire or emerald or a family-heirloom diamond, flanked by two guard rings of tiny but brilliant diamonds. And just poking out from the opened top button of the blouse—Mummy's pearls.

Their men were trim and tall. Boat shoes, khaki slacks, and navy blazers over golf shirts. Graying hair and good haircuts. To them, a neck chain was something to put on a dog.

Young couples with squirming babies were greeted by smiling grandparents. A bored attendant pushed a half-asleep dowager in an airport wheelchair.

The baggage carousel burped out leather golf bags, string-tied boxes marked Fragile, garment bags, and an assortment of suitcases that had seen better days. Bumping along in this melee was a lone Louis Vuitton suitcase that was claimed by a red-haired woman of indeterminate age in skin-tight jeans, stiletto heels, and a black T-shirt emblazoned with a hologram of a tiger's head. The golf bags were claimed by the golf people. Merry wore a nondescript business suit. One carry-on, one suitcase. The rest was being sent from New York.

Within thirty minutes, the terminal was empty.

Merry stepped outside and into a waiting taxi. The windows were open, and the warm, humid breeze wrapped around her in a phantom hug. Palm trees with swaying fronds and bright flowers—lantanas and hibiscus—filled the landscape. The fragrance wafting through the air put her in a momentary soporific daze as she smiled up at the pale blue sky with white-pillow clouds.

Warmth, beauty, and a silence that eluded Manhattan lulled her into an even deeper sense of blissful torpor. Royal Palm Way appeared as soon as the cab crossed the bridge to Palm Beach proper. Parallel rows of giant palm trees stood at regal attention in the median separating the traffic. More palm trees flanked the sundrenched buildings. Not a speck of litter in sight. On both sides of the street, pink, yellow, or sand-colored buildings stood with engraved, polished bronze signs whispering the sale of yachts, securities, real estate, and insurance. The private banks resembled embassies. So did everything else.

Rolls-Royces, Jaguars, and Mercedes-Benzes, driven by polished blondes and sleek brunettes with not one hair out of place, glided along the road with the measured speed of an ambassadorial procession. Merry could feel her limp hair frizz up in the humidity. Hopefully, a good hairdresser could fix that.

The taxi swung under the porte cochere of the Palm Crest Inn, the small hotel that Randy's office had arranged for her stay. She was more pleased than surprised as she entered the inviting foyer of this little Palm Beach gem. Randy never did anything second rate, but then, he didn't know any better.

The clerk at the front desk greeted Merry cordially. The doorman took her carry-on and led her to the elevator and her two-room suite. The fabric-covered walls created a cocoon for delicate antique furniture. A Venetian crystal chandelier hung on a velvet-covered chain from the center of the high, coffered ceiling. A desk and worktable stood in an alcove. The bedroom was exquisite. Russet, peach, and golden-apricot tones echoed the serenity and coloring of the living room. Upon entering

the bathroom, Merry was overcome by its splendor, dominated by a swan-boat-shaped tub, complete with a golden
swan waterspout. An open armoire revealed piles of soft
jade-green towels. There were bars of fragrant soaps. It
seemed more like a honeymoon suite than a place to live
for several months while decorating a new house for her
old buddy's prospective bride.

The phone rang. It was Sally from Randy's office,
inquiring if the suite was comfortable and reminding
Merry that she would be picked up by the contractor
around nine Monday morning. Would it be possible
for Merry to have some preliminary sketches ready the
following week?

Yes, the accommodations were very comfortable, and
yes, the sketches would be sent by overnight mail a week
from Monday. Sally thanked her and hung up. Merry was
on her own.

It was just after five o'clock. Too early to have dinner,
but she would enjoy a glass of wine. Off the lobby, she
found a small, softly lit mahogany bar room— the kind of
room one might find in a private dining club. Overstuffed
chairs, loveseats, and a black lacquer grand piano filled
an area just off the bar. A sense of calm and relaxation
washed over her as she held her glass while inhaling the
fragrant aromas of the deep red wine. *One hour of exposure
to the breezes of Palm Beach beats any tranquilizer,* was her only
thought.

The desk clerk suggested Vic's Place for dinner, just
two blocks away. Within five minutes, she reached her
destination. Relaxing in her seductive tub could wait
until after dinner.

The bar at Vic's Place was always crowded after the
Worth Avenue shops closed. A great place to meet for
an early evening cocktail. The din of conversations and
laughter filled the air. The dining room was in the back,

making it necessary for patrons to run a gauntlet of barstool inhabitants before reaching their destination. Women with masses of sun-bleached extension-filled hair and searching eyes that screamed, "I'm lonely," sat nursing drinks in tall glasses. The men at the bar would turn in their seats to see if they were missing anything interesting that might wiggle by on the way to the dining room. Botox and boobs. Cleavage and chin clefts. And enough porcelain on capped teeth to open a Limoges china factory.

Merry was shown to small table in a far corner of the dining room. She walked by the trolling station without being noticed. From the way everyone else was dressed, Merry, with her humidity-frizzed hair and rumpled business suit, had all the allure of an inspector from the board of health.

Dinner was an iced tea, a small salad, and freshly baked rolls. Quite unabashed because she knew no one was looking at her, Merry slipped one of the heavenly rolls into her purse.

Once outside, she took time looking into the windows of the many antique shops that lined the two short blocks to the hotel. The treasures of an Egyptian tomb would pale in comparison to the wares displayed on the tables inside the shops. Piles of silver trays were stacked as if in a cafeteria. Silver punch bowls decorated with flowers, cherubs, and birds stood next to nested teacups, dinner plates, and napkin rings. Crystal goblets crowded the glass shelves of the display cases. This was not a Palm Beach myth: it was true. When the old people died, their busy heirs, who often dined in restaurants and clubs, sold this stuff to dealers, who did them a favor by taking it off their hands. As a decorator, Merry recognized the possibilities. Some of the pieces would make great wastebaskets, soap dishes, and planters.

Later, after enjoying the hot waters of the swan-spouted bath, the fragrant soap, and the soft towels, Merry floated into twelve hours of dreamless slumber.

Bright January sunshine filled the bedroom. Merry awoke refreshed and hungry. She called the reception desk to inquire if she could have coffee, toast, and a newspaper sent up. Within ten minutes, the order was delivered. Propped up in bed, Merry called her answering service. She had received calls from both old and prospective clients. As she'd instructed, the service had informed the clients that the new La Viola team would be at their service within a few days. What she needed now was a hairdresser, and the clerk at the desk suggested one. Merry was surprised that she could get an appointment for three that afternoon.

That taken care of, Merry lazed once again among her pillows.

For the first time in years, she was a stranger. She didn't know a soul. From the time she had left Kerry Lakes to work in Boston and then moved on to New York, she always had people she knew around her. The people at Morneau's in Kerry Lakes, the people at La Viola in Boston, the Manhattan grocers, the flower-stand owners, the clerks at little Madison Avenue boutiques, and of course, her clients. Here in Palm Beach, she was in unfamiliar territory. But what a leap—from dusting furniture at Morneau's to decorating a palace in Palm Beach!

Seventeen

October 1973

Long before the demise of her invented relationship with Randy Grant, Merry already had chased away a wonderful person. His mistake was his sincerity. She kept wondering why he was so nice. *Maybe it's just an act,* she thought. She didn't really trust anyone, and she didn't want to be hurt. She could do that to herself.

"Ya see there, missy, he sees right through yoah fancy act. I told ya to act like a nahmal person, but ya have to put on that fancy act. Well, he sawr right through it and now ya know what he wants. He probably don't respect ya."

Glenda's voice, imagined as it was, hounded Merry at her every step toward social independence. As if tethered to her miserable past, Merry could not escape the nagging rebukes of her mother. But maybe her mother was right. Maybe she was out of Norm's social element.

It was Mr. Morneau who suggested that Merry should work in Boston. More opportunities, he said. In fact, he had a business acquaintance, Reno La Viola, who might consider taking her on as a trainee. Would she like that?

Merry stifled a quick, "Is the Pope Catholic?" and answered with an appreciative yes.

The first year Merry spent as an assistant to Reno La Viola was the beginning of her real training. She was attentive, a quick learner, and most of all, willing to work. "The girl has no social life," Reno said to Marion Henley, his longtime office manager.

But then Merry met someone. She was having a cup of coffee one Sunday afternoon in the lobby of the Standish Residence Hall for Women when Norm Hartwell came to visit his sister, a blue-eyed redhead whose main ambition was to be married and live in a Boston townhouse on the same street as her family. Her father had arranged for her to get a summer internship in an insurance company's underwriting department. Merry was standing by herself, looking at nothing, when Norm walked over.

"Hi, I'm Norm. Do you live here too?"

"Yes. I'm Merry." Her coffee cup and saucer shook a bit, so she placed it on a nearby end table.

"'Merry' as in a good mood?" he asked.

"Are you Norm, as in normal?"

"Is there a last name?"

"Venture. And you?"

"Hartwell."

They both laughed. He seemed nice, with his bright blue eyes, toothy smile, and a mop of unruly brown hair. She wondered if he didn't have a social life either.

They chatted for almost an hour about the kind of nothing that keeps a conversation going between strangers. "Do you know…?" "Never met them. Have you seen…?" "Not yet." It went on and on in a cycle, going nowhere, each participant waiting for encouragement from the other, a signal to move on.

Finally, an awkward pause, which Norm filled. "I was planning to have an early dinner at Howard Johnson's and see a movie. Join me? You're not busy, are you? If you are, maybe we could go another time."

"But I'm hungry now. Who knows when the next pang of hunger will strike? Could be years."

"I'll just tell Betsy we're leaving."

"Betsy?"

"My sister. Over there talking to those girls. Do you know them?"

Hardly, she thought. *They are the type of girls who wouldn't give me the time of day.* "I haven't met too many people yet. I work long hours."

"Come on, I'll introduce you."

They walked across the large, open lobby. Merry's heartbeat quickened uncomfortably.

"Betsy, I'd like you to meet Merry Venture."

"Nice to meet you. Do you live here?"

"Yes."

"These are my friends, Caroline and Brooke. They live here too."

The women exchanged greetings.

"What floor do you live on?" Betsy asked, obviously not interested, only being polite.

"Three."

"I'm on five. You should come up sometime and meet some of my floor mates."

"I will."

Silence—the kind that results from an unsuccessful encounter.

"I'll go upstairs, Norm, and get my purse." Merry wondered if the dinner would be Dutch, or if he would pay for the whole thing.

The early fall evening was cool. She was cold inside, chilled by the thought that she might have been too eager to accept Norm's invitation. What did those girls think of her? What did he think of her?

Norm paid for both the dinner and the movie. After the movie they stopped off at Bramley's for brownies à la

mode with hot fudge as thick as melted tar and as delicious as a taste of heaven. Merry was back at Standish
by ten. Norm said good-bye and disappeared into the
evening fog.

At least it was a sort of date, Merry thought as she got
ready for the bed. But the next day she forgot all about it,
too excited by a new work project. Reno gave her a pile
of floor plans and told her to transform them into room
sketches. They were for a variety of Newton matrons and
Brookline newlyweds whose self-images depended on
how much they could impress their friends with country-French furniture, lamps made from electrified tin
milk cans, area rugs, and flocked wallpaper. The Hyannis
summer people always insisted on good, sturdy striped
ticking slipcovers. For the daring, there were darling
prints with ducks or sailboats.

One evening two weeks later, Norm called. "Busy?"
he asked.

"Terribly. I was reading a magazine. What about you?"

"I've been in New York at an investment seminar.
When I got back, I had to write my report."

"Sounds exciting." Merry hadn't a clue what Norm
was talking about. "What else is new?"

"Well, I got a raise. I thought we could go over to the
Eliot Lounge for a celebration cocktail."

"And when will this event take place?"

"Right now, if you like. I can pick you up. I've got
Dad's Chevy."

Let's hope it's not a flatbed truck, Merry thought. Her
answer was more demure. "How about picking me up
around seven thirty?"

"See you then."

"I'll be downstairs."

The Eliot Lounge was just dark enough to make the rather shabby room look romantic. Small sofas and loveseats filled the room. Each little round table had cocktail napkins and a glass bowl of potato chips. A few peanuts were mixed in.

Merry had never been anywhere like this. As she looked around the semi-darkened room, she saw young couples chatting quietly. The girls sipped Brandy Alexanders or champagne cocktails. The men nursed scotch and sodas. One did not drink beer at the Eliot Lounge. As her eyes adjusted to the dim light, Merry realized how awful she looked. Sitting around the room were the cashmere-sweater-set young ladies, legs crossed at the ankles, feet encased in Capezio flats or little Louis heels from Joseph Antel. Merry was beginning to feel hot and sweaty. A great drop of perspiration rolled down her side and deposited itself at the waistband of her underwear. Then Merry felt chilly. Why had she ever agreed to go out? Ever?

"Is something the matter?" Norm asked.

"Everything's fine. I think I'm getting eyestrain from all the sketches I've been making." She rubbed her eyes and then squirmed in her chair.

"You're an artist?"

"I'm a decorator trainee at La Viola."

"Mr. La Viola did our summer cottage at Hyannis and all of my aunt's houses and my dad's offices."

The waitress brought their drinks, and Merry sipped in this information along with the sweet-tasting drink. "You know where I live, but I don't know where you live."

"Just around the corner, really. On Beacon Street, between Clarendon and Dartmouth. Where are you from?"

An innocent question, but it had the shattering power of a wrecking ball on a plate-glass window.

"New Hampshire. Kerry Lakes. And please don't say 'Merry from Kerry.'"

"Actually, I was going to say something else."

"Like what?"

"Like, how would you like to go out for dinner next week? Maybe to Joseph's?"

"Is it dressy?" That was the only thing Merry could think of to say.

"I don't know. I've never worn a dress."

They both laughed.

In silence, they enjoyed the moment. Merry took a long sip of her intoxicating drink and relaxed. When Norm drove her back to the Standish, she decided that her champagne cocktail had been wonderful. She even felt a bit woozy. And she had had a good time.

The next day, the office manager at La Viola went into a state of near shock when Merry asked if she could take an afternoon off. Not once had Merry ever asked for anything.

"Are you feeling sick?" Marion Henley asked.

"Well, no. There's a sale at Conrad's basement, and I want to get a dress. Is it all right?"

"A dress? At Conrad's? In the basement?" Had Marion said, "What? You have typhoid?", her tone of voice could not have conveyed more surprise. Quickly recovering, she said in a motherly way, "Go down the street to Sabian's. My sister works there. I'll call her, and she'll take care of you."

"Sabian's? That sounds wonderful, but it's so expensive."

"Don't worry. Ask for Loretta. And take the rest of the day off." Marion dialed the phone. "Loretta? Back from lunch?"

Eighteen

Across the street from the Boston Commons, on the corner of Arlington and Newberry Streets, the shoes and handbags displayed in the windows of Joseph Antel were as tasteful as the window displays of the gemstones and silver tureens at Shreve, Crump & Low. At the beginning of each season, a procession of debs and dowagers entered through the polished glass doors of Joseph Antel to stock up on shoes. It was the only place a woman could buy shoes that matched a dress purchased on Newberry Street.

On Newberry Street itself, each of the two windows of Sabian's dress shop featured only one dress. Always one style in one color, with Sabian's signature organza flower that started at the shoulder and ended in a trailing satin vine at the hem. It was not the kind of place where one went "just to look."

Merry opened the heavy glass door and entered the shop. It was a quiet establishment. No counters and no decorations. Just dresses that hung on ivory linen dressmaker forms. As Merry came in, she was greeted by a woman who looked very much like Marion Henley.

"I'm Loretta Conroy, Marion's sister. You must be Merry. Take off your coat, and let's get started."

Merry let her coat slip off and placed it on a chair.

"What a lovely figure you have! I know just the dress for you." Loretta disappeared into the back of the store and returned carrying a garment bag. "This one is going to be our bestseller with the younger crowd at holiday time. It's a new design." Loretta unzipped the bag and presented the dress—a simple long-sleeved sheath dress of fine wool crepe in sapphire blue. At the waist, a thin sapphire-blue satin belt clasped with a sapphire-blue organza rose completed the creation.

Merry couldn't take her eyes off the dress. It was lovely.

"Try it on. It's a sample."

A few minutes later, Merry emerged from the fitting room wearing the dress. She was glowing.

"It's perfect on you. You could model this dress. Do you like it?"

"I love it. But I don't think I can afford anything like this. I was looking for something on sale."

Kindly, Loretta informed Merry that Sabian's did not have sales. "This dress isn't for sale. It's a new sample. But we want you to wear it for Sabian's wherever you go this season, so it will get more exposure than just being the holiday dress in the window."

Loretta said this with such assurance that Merry's ego got a much-needed boost. Of course, Merry did not know that Marion had called Loretta and asked her for a special favor—that she give a dress to this rather hapless young woman. It was not a strain to grant the request, as Marion occasionally gave Loretta a sample coffee table or a pair of lamps, with Reno's permission. Merry was overwhelmed. The last time she had received a gift had been three years ago, when Mrs. Morneau gave her that Martha Washington bedspread for graduation.

"I have a dinner date next week at Joseph's."

"Joseph's is wonderful. It's so elegant. Everyone goes there."

"Thank you for the dress and your help. I just love it." Merry gave Loretta an appreciative hug and then kissed her on the cheek.

Back in the fitting room, Loretta helped Merry out of the dress and returned it to the garment bag. "Wear the dress at La Viola. It's good advertising for us."

"After my date, I will. How much is this dress, anyway?"

"As I said, it's a sample. Just enjoy it, because on you, it looks like a million."

With the garment bag over her arm, Merry headed for Joseph Antel. Just once, she would splurge.

The dress-shop experience awakened in Merry the realization that her drab Kerry Lakes wardrobe was indeed shabby, and it made her feel shabby. Imbued with the flush of the revelation, she vowed that her life would change. She didn't know how this would happen, just that it would.

For once, she felt she looked beautiful. The gods were with her. Every hair was in place, and her new shoes did not pinch.

Norm didn't have to wait long for her to emerge from the elevator when he came to pick her up. He couldn't believe his eyes.

"You look beautiful, Merry." He put his arm around her as he escorted her out the door to a chauffeur-driven Cadillac limousine.

Merry said nothing. *What's going on? Who is this guy?*

Once in the car, Norman directed Stevens, the chauffeur, to drive to Joseph's.

The black car took off on the five-minute ride. *Boston looks so beautiful from a limousine,* Merry thought.

Joseph's. Sedate. White tablecloths. Attentive service. Elegant clientele. Merry looked around the softly lit dining room as the maître d' guided them to their table.

"Good to see you again, Mr. Hartwell. I'll send Maurice over. He'll take care of you this evening. May I suggest the trout? It is excellent tonight." He pulled a chair from the table for Merry.

A waiter slipped a napkin onto her lap and placed a menu before her. Everything was in French. There were no prices.

"This is my favorite place," Norm said. "I hope you like it."

"Yes, I do. It's very elegant."

Her eyes became sponges, absorbing the rarified atmosphere. Never in her life had she been in a place like this. It looked like a movie scene, only she was in it. The low hum of discreet conversations came from the surrounding tables. Small candles under delicate crystal shades caused diamond earrings, pins, and rings to sparkle like prisms. Strings of pearls glowed with the patina of delicate satin. Everyone looked like they belonged.

Merry wore no jewelry. It was not a choice. She did not own any, not even a Kerry Lakes High School class ring.

"Shall we order now," Norm asked, "or would you like an aperitif first?"

"That would be nice. I never ate one, even before supper."

Instantly, her mother's voice intruded. *"My, my, ahrn't we fancy. Why don't ya just tell him ya've never been anywheah like this?"*

Mother, you are not invited here.

"What's the mattah? Ashamed?"

Please leave me alone.

"You look deep in thought," Norm said.

"Not really. Just enjoying the moment."

"And the company?" He flashed his great wide smile.

"Yes. Yes, I am."

"What would you like?"

"You order. I know I'll like whatever you choose."

After their aperitifs, Maurice presented their trout and skillfully boned it tableside. The salad was definitely not a wedge of mayonnaise-covered iceberg lettuce, and the dessert tart was filled with succulent raspberries nestling in a custard sauce.

"I don't think I'll be able to eat the stuff they serve at the Standish anymore."

Norm reached across the table and took her hand. "Merry, I'd like to get to know you better. What do you think?"

"I think it would be nice." But she was aware of the hesitancy in her voice, even if he wasn't.

"Let's go for a drive. Any place special?"

"Why don't you choose."

This was almost too much. Perhaps she should just ask to go home. But before she could suggest that, Norm asked, "Isn't there anything you ever choose?"

"Not often, but I will let you know when I do."

The bill was presented in a leather folder. Norm signed it and handed it back to the waiter. "It was a good dinner, Maurice." Merry noted that "dinner" was preferred to "supper."

As they left the restaurant, Norm put his arm around Merry. She could smell the faint aroma of his aftershave as he drew her closer to him. Almost reflexively, she stiffened in his casual embrace.

"Did I do something wrong?" he asked.

"No, of course not." Her voice weak, she asked if he could take her back to the Standish. She couldn't call it home, because she did not have one. A headache was coming on. She was frightened because she didn't know what was expected of her. The headache intensified as the internal wrestling match with her emotions held her in a tight grip.

The limousine pulled up to the door of the Standish. A couple of girls just entering the building stopped to see who was in the long black vehicle. When the driver helped Merry out of the backseat, the girls' eyes almost popped out of their heads.

When they got to the door, Norm stopped and took Merry by the shoulders. "Merry, is there something wrong? Won't you tell me what it is? Did I say something?"

"It's nothing like that, honestly. It's just that…" Tears fell from her eyes as she stood frozen to the spot.

"I didn't mean any more than that it would be nice if we knew each other better. Nothing more than that. Okay?"

"Okay."

"I'll call you tomorrow."

The moment was over. A ruined evening. *He only says he'll call. He's too polite to just say good-bye.* Merry took the elevator up to her cubicle, a room little bigger than a prison cell. She recalled seeing a photograph of a women's prison in one of the tabloid newspapers. *What crime did I commit?*

The headache declared its superiority over her as she took off her dress and crawled into bed. Her sleep was fitful, leaving her exhausted in the morning.

Nineteen

November 1973

"Looks like somebody had a good time last night," Reno said when Merry got to work the next day. "This came for you before we opened." He handed her a long box with the unmistakable stamp of Quint's, Boston's best florist. "Aren't you going to open it?"

Merry pushed aside the tissue that concealed a dozen yellow roses. The card was simple: *Merry, I'll call for you after work.*

"Anyone special?" Reno loved to know things, especially of the romantic nature.

"Just a friend."

"Oh, I see. Just a friend."

Merry smiled, but her head had begun to pound again. "We've been out a couple of times. That's really all there is to it."

"Merry, dear heart, since you are alone here in Boston, always feel free to talk to me. Just think of me as your fairy godfather. Well, you know what I mean."

"I do, and thank you." She went to put the bouquet in water. By the time she was finished, Reno was on the phone with a client.

Once she was absorbed in her sketches, Merry's headache disappeared. When she finally looked up at the clock, it was almost closing time. She'd forgotten to eat lunch. And in a few minutes, Norm would be picking her up. Maybe she should allow herself to be happy.

Reno poked his head into her little work space. "Merry, there is someone to see you. You can finish the rest tomorrow."

"I'll be right there." She gathered her purse and coat and went to meet her date.

Norm greeted her and suggested they finish the drive they were going to take the previous night.

"Where to?"

"Just across the river to Memorial Drive. We can talk there."

"Sounds good to me."

The sun had set, and it was beginning to get dark. The vibrant activity of shoppers was replaced with clumps of dour-faced office workers and salesgirls scurrying into the dark oblivion of the MTA.

Norm opened the door to a small foreign-looking car. Even Merry could recognize an MG.

"Hop in." Norm made a slight bow, all the while smiling at Merry.

In silence they headed up Massachusetts Avenue, but it was an awkward silence, the kind reserved for those who were not quite certain what the outcome would be if they spoke. The view from across the bridge offered a spectacular panorama of Back Bay in the fading twilight. Suddenly, an eerie sensation of isolation enveloped Merry, so that she felt as if she were the sole inhabitant of the planet. She looked at the townhouses they passed, where the occasional glow of soft amber and yellow lights in the windows pierced the oncoming darkness. The chilled air promised that winter would soon blanket everything with snow. *Enjoy it now,* whispered the fallen leaves as they were swept along by the invisible broom of the wind.

Norm pulled up to the curb. A ribbon of cars stretched along the curbside; apparently other couples had things to talk about too.

"Merry, please don't say anything until I finish. It's not much, but..."

"Okay," she said tentatively.

"It's like this. I like you, but I don't know a thing about you. And you don't know a thing about me. I'd like us to get to know each other better and take it from there, but sometimes you seem so far way. Is there someone else, or should I continue? Merry?"

For what seemed like an eternity, Merry tried to absorb that brief but seemingly sincere overture. What should she say? How should she act? With hesitation, she replied, "I guess so. I mean, I really hadn't thought about this. At least, the way I think you mean. But I'd like to get to know you better."

He took her hand in his and gently pulled her toward him. The gearshift box got in the way. They started laughing. Norm got out of the car and opened Merry's door.

Extending his hand, he urged her out of the car and pulled her to him. He kissed her, gently at first. It was a sweet kiss. Then he pulled her even closer and kissed her again, arousing a passion she had never felt before.

"Merry, I think I'm falling in love with you." He kissed her again.

"I don't know what to say."

"I don't want you to say anything."

They stood in silence, arm in arm, looking out over the moon-bathed Charles River.

"Are you hungry?" Norm asked.

"No, but coffee would be nice."

"But you haven't had dinner."

"I'm not hungry, really."

"Let's go someplace near you."

"Great."

"How about some pie? Can I talk you into some pie?"

"Only if it's à la mode."

They exchanged a friendly kiss... and a new relationship formed. The kisses and the relationship were Merry's first, and she tried to allow herself the permission to be happy.

During the next three weeks, Norm called Merry every evening that they weren't out together. They went to the movies or dinner, took long walks through the Commons, went window shopping. Sometimes, they talked about nothing and just walked hand in hand in mutual comfort.

For those three weeks, Merry transformed herself from what she felt was a plain Kerry Lakes kind of girl into her version of an elegant Back Bay swan. She spent most of her salary on new clothes—yet in her mind, each new purchase turned into a rag the minute she put it on.

Merry tried on a new London Ladies dress in her little room and looked at her reflection in the full-length mirror on the wall. She affected an unattractive, slumped pose, making herself look perfectly wretched.

"So ya think ya can fool people with yoah new clothes? Well, let me tell ya something, missy—they'ah on to ya. Ya shoulda stayed in Kerry Lakes, wheah ya belong."

Who needs to stay in Kerry Lakes to be near you? You seem to have no trouble following me wherever I am, was Merry's unspoken response.

Unzipping the newest London Ladies dress, she took it off, carefully folded it, and placed it back in the pink box. She would return it tomorrow. When she returned from her solitary dinner in the cafeteria, she reopened the box, pushed aside the tissue paper, and hung the dress back in the closet. *Why not keep it? I didn't steal it. I paid for it.* During the time Merry and Norm were dating, they kept to themselves. It did not occur to Merry that young people usually were surrounded by lots of friends. But they were gradually learning about each other. Norm didn't ask too many questions about Merry's family; he let her offer what she felt important at the moment. And he spoke warmly of his. They were just having fun.

One Thursday in November, Merry was surprised to find a letter in her mailbox. Although she looked in the box every day, it was always empty. Who would write to her? She looked at the pale gray envelope. Turning it over, she saw the fine script announcing that it was from Norm's house.

She opened the envelope and drew out a small pale-gray folded note card with three initials embossed in white in the center. Had she known about stationery and held it to the light, she would have seen the Tiffany water-mark.

Dear Merry,

Please join me for tea at four o'clock this Sunday. I am looking forward to meeting you.

Sincerely,
Caroline Maynard Hartwell
(Mrs. Thomas)

The telephone number was enclosed on an engraved calling card.

Merry decided to respond to the invitation and call Mrs. Hartwell.

"Hartwell residence. Whom shall I say is calling?" The voice had a slight British clip.

"Merry Venture. May I speak with Mrs. Hartwell?"

"Mrs. Hartwell is not at home. Do you wish to leave a message?"

"Yes. Please tell her that Merry Venture accepts her invitation for tea on Sunday."

"Merry Venture? Yes, your name is on the list."

"You won't forget to tell her?"

"Good day, Miss Venture."

What does it mean? Merry wondered as she hung up. Why would Norm's mother invite her? Who else would be there? What would she say to people? This unexpected invitation loosed a blizzard of fears. Merry felt choked as she sat on her bed and studied the invitation, as if hidden meanings lurked between the lines.

"An invitation to a house on Beacon Street?" Glenda said. *"Tea, no less. Well, ahrn't we the fancy one. Let's see how fah them ayhers take you now, missy."*

The invitation was addressed to me, not you, Mother.

"Don't put on that fancy accent with me. They'll see phony the minute ya get theah."

Thank you for your kind words. My God, I don't even have to be at home to hear your messages. I'm on automatic pilot.

The only time Merry ever drank tea was when she was sick or had terrible period cramps, so for her, tea was always associated with something unpleasant. Who would drink tea when they were feeling well? Then she remembered the times she had sat in the dark of Kerry Lakes' movie house, watching scenes of "rich people" wearing exquisite afternoon dresses, hats, and furs, sipping tea while a uniformed maid passed a tray of dainty sandwiches from guest to guest. The extravagant settings always were filled with beautiful furniture and large French doors that opened out to a terrace view of a lake or a fountain. But this real invitation was not a fantasy of a lone girl sitting in a darkened theater, accompanied by a box of popcorn.

What will I wear? What will I say? "Hi? How do you do?"
Merry knew from watching B movies that nice girls never
said, "Charmed, I'm sure." *Maybe I should just say, "What a
lovely invitation." No, that's no good. How about "Thank you
for inviting me"?*

*Who knows? Maybe she's a drunk, and when she gets up
from her chair to greet me, she falls over and passes out. No, she
won't get out of her chair—she'll sit there like a queen, extending
her arm covered with diamond bracelets that extend down to the
emerald rings on her old, gnarled, cane-clutching fingers.*

*Come on, Merry, you know she'll be a smart-looking woman
in an expensive dress, and she'll give you that withering, sympa-
thetic look so well expressed by on-screen grande dames, like Mary
Astor, who disapprove of their son's "little friends."*

Tea on Sunday? She wasn't going any day. Suddenly,
Merry felt a headache overtaking her and decided to lie
down and sleep for a while.

When she awoke the next morning, she was fully
clothed. Even her shoes were still on. She recalled what
had put her in such a state. Fear. Fear of a dream that
became reality. Fear of being exposed as Merry from Railroad Street.

But since she wasn't going, she had nothing to worry
about.

With that determination in mind, she got up and
started the day without any further thought about Sunday.

It was Friday, and Merry had a couple of hours to
shop before the stores closed. The area that extended as
far as Washington Street was in another universe across
the Commons, where large department stores, furriers,
and jewelry shops attracted shop girls and office workers
on their lunch hours. They scurried in and out of these
places, like bees around a hive. They were in the land
of *easy payments.* The young women wore the ambivalent

expression of desire for the perfect dress and the desperation of trying to pay for it.

London Ladies Styles would have been at home on Washington Street, but the owners were wise enough to locate on Boylston Street, which was just that much closer to Newberry Street. The salesgirls at London Ladies imitated the women who were employed in the exclusive shops on Newberry Street.

Merry was now considered a regular customer. She even had her own salesgirls who knew just what she liked. When Louise suggested that Merry open a charge account, Merry felt flattered. Of course, Louise got one dollar for every new account she opened.

On this particular Friday, after Merry charged several outfits, Louise asked if she would like to meet her and some of the girls for a drink and dinner at Romero's after the store closed. Merry accepted the invitation and walked back to the Standish to put on one of her new outfits for the evening.

Romero's was the place for the best lasagna, the best wine, and the best desserts, according to Louise's friends, Bunny and Helen. They both worked at the pharmacy not far from the Standish.

"You never sawr us there?" Bunny asked in her thick Boston accent, which added *R*s where they didn't belong and dropped them at other places. "I'm at the cosmetics counta." Bunny said this as she studied the menu, carefully looking at the price column before making her choice, which would, as always, be lasagna.

Bunny was a short young woman with all the tendencies toward a premature middle-aged spread. At twenty-three, she was just beginning to look older than her age. Since she worked at the cosmetic counter, she sampled all the newest makeup and hair colorings. That night, her swirling, dyed-black hairdo looked like a burned Danish pastry surrounding her overly powdered face, which featured a brilliantly painted red mouth and eyelids done in shadow tones that would make a parrot look anemic. The total effect was of a little girl playing with her mother's cosmetics.

In contrast, Helen was plain, flat-chested, slightly buck-toothed, and scrawny, a nondescript person who worked the women's feminine hygiene products counter. No one would ever feel embarrassed asking Helen for a bottle of douche.

Bunny and Helen were the same age, and both were engaged to be married the following June. Each girl wore an engagement ring containing a microscopic diamond. This style was part of the Heirloom Collection, emblazoned on advertising banners in the windows of the Washington Street jewelry stores, along with "Twelve Months, No Down Payment."

Louise was going to get engaged over Christmas and then get married two years later. She and Ryan were saving for a really big wedding. Louise was by far the most attractive of the three women, which accounted for her slightly superior way of describing her employment as an "assistant fashion consultant." Her work outfit was a black dress and a string of fake pearls. Her version of fashion-model makeup was sweeping false eyelashes, pencil-line eyebrows, and a puff of stiffly sprayed, over-bleached blonde hair that rested on her head like a helmet.

In this company, Merry felt at ease. She was actually enjoying herself. And after a glass of wine, everyone was in a relaxed mood and acting like old friends.

"Merry, you're really one of us. Right, girls?" Louise said. She was clearly the leader of the group.

Bunny and Helen chimed in agreement. Everyone ordered a second glass of wine. Everyone ordered lasagna.

The wine relaxed Bunny into a state of friendly concern for this virtual stranger. "You know, Merry, my cousin Rosalie is getting married tomorrow, and she said for me to bring along another girl because her cousin Arlene can't come. I'd like you to come to the service and the reception. You could meet some nice guys. Who knows? Maybe you'll get engaged too."

"You should come," Louise said. "It'll be nice. I know Rosalie would like it. And yeah, you might meet someone special." Louise gave this pronouncement under the glow of the two very large glasses of wine.

"I don't know," Merry said. "You hardly know me. Anyway, I don't have a present to give them."

"Don't worry about that," Helen said. "We all chipped in five dollahs and bought them a coffee makah. We could put your name on the cahd too."

"I'd like that, but are you sure I wouldn't be a third wheel?"

Louise assured Merry that she would be more than welcome.

"Where is this wedding?"

"In South Boston, the Crystal Palace Banquet Hall. Eleven o'clock. Do you know where that is?"

Bunny smiled. A piece of lasagna rested on her chin. "You could get a ride with my aunt Mary Grace," Bunny said. "She lives near you. I'll go call her now. So, you'll come?"

Merry looked at the smeared lasagna on Bunny's face. "I'd love to. Sounds like fun."

Helen accompanied Bunny to the phone and back. "Well, it's all fixed up. My aunt will pick you up."

That settled, the rest of the evening was devoted to talking about wedding plans, getting pregnant right away, and what kind of furniture they would buy. And how great the meal tasted! The aroma of Romero's garlic rolls!

That first bite of pure oily ecstasy. Who could possibly have room for the biscuit tortoni? Merry had nothing to offer to this conversation, but she wondered silently why she couldn't be happy like these women.

"Merry, what are you thinking?" Helen asked. "You're so quiet." Helen had just passed her engagement ring around for everyone to examine.

"I was wondering if I would catch the bouquet."

It was almost ten o'clock when the little group left the restaurant. The other women decided to walk Merry back to the Standish, and then they'd take the MTA to their respective homes from there. Merry felt as if she belonged; she was like them. Her new friends were nobodies, just like her. This Norm business was just foolishness. Who did she think she was?

When Merry got back to the Standish, she found a message in her mail slot. It was from Norm. *Merry, I'll pick you up at 7:00 tomorrow night and 3:30 on Sunday afternoon. Norm.*

Merry looked at the message and then crumpled it up and dropped it into the trash basket in the hall.

Sorry, she told him silently. *I'm not going out on Saturday, and I am not attending the inspection on Sunday.*

The decision was made. Merry now was traveling on a path that felt familiar. Louise, Bunny, and Helen reminded her of the people in Kerry Lakes. Ordinary people who did ordinary things. Nothing fancy. No champagne cocktails or limousines. And no inspection teas.

Twenty

November 1973

The only weddings Merry had ever seen were the ones on the screen in the little movie house in Kerry Lakes. The brides always looked like princesses in satin and lace gowns. The bouquets of roses, orchids, and stephanotises cascaded from the hands of these young women as they walked demurely down the aisle with distinguished-looking fathers who were usually bankers, governors, or millionaires. The grooms waited at the altar, eyes filled with love, respect, and admiration. The music, the toasts, the European honeymoon—and then the pretty little house with an ivy trellis and a picket fence. *The End.*

The ride to Rosalie's wedding was mostly in silence. Bunny's aunt Mary Grace was busy driving and feeling inside her dress to push her sagging shoulder pads back up. "These things can be so dahn annoying." That was the extent of the conversation. The heavy aroma of cheap perfume clung to the air, dragging with it a whiff of talcum powder and the suggestion of perspiration. Merry wished she could open the windows but thought better of asking.

As they continued toward their destination, she observed that many of the wooden tenements resembled versions of her Railroad Street house stacked one on top of the other—shabby, dreary, even under the sunny, cloudless sky. Among these dwellings loomed the Crystal Palace.

Bridesmaids and ushers were gathered outside, while family, friends, children, and old people made their way into the Palace. Aunt Mary Grace wedged her car into the last available spot in the lot across the street.

"Hold this for me?" She shoved a large package wrapped in wedding paper into Merry's arms. Merry wondered if Mary Grace was giving the happy couple a bag of cement as she struggled across the street, trying not to drop the gift. Mary Grace was busy retrieving her dislodged shoulder pads, which had now slipped down to her waist.

Merry was shown to a seat in the back of the chapel-like room. Bunny, Helen, and their fiancés, along with Louise and her boyfriend, were seated a couple of rows in front of her.

Bunny turned around and pointed at the heavy-looking man in his early twenties beside her. "Psst, Merry. We'll be sitting together at the reception. This is Bill. A real hunk, huh?"

The portable organ filled the room with wedding music. A little flower girl appeared carrying a pink satin basket from which she heaved clumps of paper rose petals down the aisle. The ring bearer trudged after her, balancing a pillow to which the ring was pinned. Both children were dressed in purple velvet and violet lace. The girl's dress was decorated with pink bows, while the boy's lace-collared Lord Fauntleroy-style suit was tied at the neck, wrists, and knees with blue satin bows. Both children wore white stockings and purple satin shoes trimmed with the appropriate-color bows.

"How cute," echoed around the pews.

His Cuteness stuck out his tongue.

As the organ pumped out the bridal theme, six bridesmaids appeared in hoop-skirted, puffed-sleeved satin gowns, each one in a different color: pale pink, sky blue, lavender, green, yellow, and peach. Bouquets of carnations and roses, sprayed to match their gowns, and large garden-party–style hats completed the theme of a Rainbow Wedding.

With a loud fanfare, Rosalie and her father, in his too-tight rented tuxedo, started down the aisle. The bride's dress was a hoop-covered tulle affair, lavished with lace, bows, and little velvet flowers and sprinkled with iridescent spangles. Merry thought the bride looked like a giant lampshade and wondered if there was a string to pull to light her up. Murmurs rose through the assembled guests. "She looks so beautiful." "The perfect bride." "Her flowers are gorgeous." A stout young woman in a tight red satin dress remarked, "If the bouquet were any larger, you'd think she'd won a horse race." Merry found out later that the woman in the red dress was the bride's unmarried cousin.

After the ceremony, the bride and groom kissed and then sprinted down the aisle to the banquet hall, with the wedding party close behind.

The banquet hall was decorated with yards of white tulle, paper wedding bells, and white crepe-paper streamers. A long-skirted head table was festooned with tulle bows, more paper wedding bells, and more streamers, with the names of the bride and groom printed in gold. Commanding a round table was a six-tier wedding cake adorned with a rainbow of frosting swags, hearts, cupids, and rosebud sprays. Pools of silver frosting decorated with swans filled the spaces under each of the four columns on each of the tiers. The top of the cake was crowned with a miniature bride and groom, sitting in a swan boat covered with pink rosebuds. The swan wore a miniature rhinestone tiara that matched the headdress of the bride. Merry overheard someone say that it was the Eternal Paradise Wedding Cake, the signature creation of Malucci's Bakery.

Bunny, Helen, and Louise rushed over to Merry, all talking at once. Louise took Merry by the hand. "We're going to sit at that table over there. The guys are getting the beer."

Bunny, not one to let Louise run the whole show, stepped in. "Come on. You'll meet Connie and Brian. They just started going out. And Pete Mercer is sitting with us, too. He's nice. You'll like him."

The girls sat at a table, waiting for the guys to come back with pitchers of beer. When they arrived, Louise introduced Pete and Merry and told Pete to sit beside her.

"I'll move over so we can sit boy-girl," Helen added.

Introductions and awkward conversation limped around the table as each of the young people attempted to ward off the dreaded awkward silence.

A three-piece band played the first number for the bride and groom. The groom tried to steer the bride around the room as she hung on to him as if he were a life raft. She was saved. And she wasn't showing.

Pete stood up, slicked back his hair, and straightened his tie. "Wanna dance?" he asked Merry.

"Sure." Merry really wasn't sure she even wanted to be there, let alone dance.

"I never sawr you around here. Where you from?"

"I live at the Standish in Boston."

"Za' righ'? I thought you might be some kinda debutante, the way you dressed."

"Really?" Merry was at a loss for words.

"Yeah. The girls around here don't go too much for plain dresses. So that's what I thought."

"No, it's just a regular dinner dress."

"So, how do you know Bunny, Helen, and Louise?"

The song ended and the emcee announced that the buffet was being served.

"I think we'd better sit down," Merry said, hoping to end the interrogation.

"So you've been friends for long?" Pete ran his tongue over the corner of his lower lip.

"Seems like that."

Satisfied with Merry's reply, Pete went on. "Wanna get some eats?" He steered her toward the long buffet tables. Metal steam trays were filled with lasagna, sausage and peppers, meatballs, fried chicken, vegetables in a sauce, and a salad of chopped iceberg lettuce sprinkled with shaved carrots and pale tomato slices. Other trays were piled with sandwiches, both ham and roast beef. Platters of assorted cold cuts, rolls, and potato salad blanketed the second table. The third table contained ice-filled tubs of soda and a huge beer keg surrounded with glass pitchers. That table attracted the men.

The afternoon dragged on. Conversations were laced with raucous, beer-induced frivolity. Louise and her boyfriend left early. "We know where you're going," Bunny said to Helen, giggling. Connie and Brian excused themselves to sit with some of Brian's friends. A drum roll summoned everyone to watch the bride and groom cut the cake. Flashbulbs snapped as guests took pictures. A waiter rolled the cake table to the kitchen. The brides-maids walked from table to table, distributing tiny white boxes to hold pieces of the cake "to dream on." After coffee was served, the bride threw her bouquet. The cousin in the tight red dress lunged for it, beating out all the other hopefuls.

One by one, guests wished the newlyweds good luck, and then the bride and groom were off to start their new life. It was 3:30 p.m., and Merry couldn't find Aunt Mary Grace. How was she to get home?

"I can give you a ride back," Pete said. "I'm going that way anyway." He lit a cigarette and offered one to Merry.

She refused the cigarette but accepted the ride. She wished she had another way to get back, but she didn't, so out of necessity she remained pleasant.

A cold wind and slight drizzle added to the sadness of the neighborhood. Like tears. Merry choked back her own tears. A day wasted, with people whose friendship had been the result of a casual dinner and two glasses of wine the night before. The hopeful feeling she had had just hours earlier had dissolved, reappearing as a picture of a future she prayed would not come true. She had no one in her life. Would she ever? She breathed in the chilly air. *This is what I deserve. It's true. I was putting on airs. Mother was right. Who do I think I am?*

"Here's the car, doll. Get in." Pete let Merry open the door for herself. "You want some smokes?"

"No, thank you, I don't smoke."

"Tha's ri', you told me that before. It's nicer when a girl don't. Makes her look more refined. Ya know what I mean? That's what I thought when I first sawr you. I thought, 'She looks refined.' I'm not embarrassing you, am I?"

"No, not at all." Merry sat as close to the car door as possible. She felt cornered.

"Wanna get a coffee or something? I feel like a coffee. You?"

"Sure, why not? Coffee sounds good." Why did she say that? It seemed to be spoken by someone outside herself.

The neighborhood doughnut shop was as sad and shabby as the tenement houses that lined the street. They sat at the counter, the pungent odor of the floor having just been washed with bleach assaulted Merry's senses. Pete ordered two coffees. "Wanna doughnut?"

"Do they have glazed?"

"Two glazed doughnuts," he told the woman behind the counter.

Merry was at a loss for conversation. All she could think about were the events of the afternoon. Was it a preview of her life? But why was she sitting here with someone she didn't know and didn't care about? What was the matter with her?

"Goin' with anyone?" Pete took a long drag on the cigarette and let the smoke curl out of his nose.

"Not right now."

"Then there was someone?"

"A long time ago." Merry felt comfortable with that explanation.

"It's still early. Wanna go for a drive?"

"Where to?" And why had she said that? Did it sound as if she were leading him on?

"Just around." He lit another cigarette.

"I think I'd better go back now. I still have some work to do for tomorrow."

"What kinda work?" Pete took a long drag on his cigarette.

"I work for an interior decorator. I do the sketches. And you?"

"I'm kinda between jobs. I was workin' for a construction company, but it didn't work out."

Back in his car, they drove in silence for a few minutes. Pete lit another cigarette. "Sure you don't want one?"

"No, but thank you just the same."

He steered the car into a lonely area of deserted warehouses, stopped the car, and put out his cigarette.

"Where are we?" Merry asked.

"It's a nice place to talk."

She wondered what she should say as Pete slid over to her. He put his arm around her and yanked her toward him. Then he kissed her, parting her lips with his tongue. His hand crept up her dress. Merry was caught in an embrace, and it was strangling her. She had never felt like this before. She felt like throwing up—like retching in total disgust with herself.

"Babe, this is your first time, isn't it?"

"Yes." Her stomach was turning. All she wanted to do was get out of there. "I don't feel too well. I'm going to be sick." She wasn't lying, either.

"You shoulda told me."

"I want to go back." Tears of shame fell from her eyes as she realized she'd sunk to the level of her expectations. Why was she with this creep? Just how much did she need to punish herself?

"Okay. Suit yourself." Pete lit another cigarette and started the car. "Sure you want to go back?"

"Yes. I'm really feeling sick."

"It wasn't because I made a move on you? If you didn't want it, you shoulda said so."

"It's just that I'm feeling really sick."

"Suit yourself."

They drove in silence. Pete looked deep in thought. "Do you want to go out sometime? We could take it slow, if you want."

"Right now, all I can think about is getting back to the Standish and throwing up."

Pete had barely stopped in front of the Standish when Merry bolted from the car. She ran into the lobby, heading straight for the elevator. As the elevator ascended, she started to unzip her dress so that she could get out of it as soon as she got into her room. Once there, she ripped off all her clothes and shoved them into the wastebasket, put on her robe, grabbed her towel, and ran to the common bathroom to shower off the day.

Not long after she returned to her room, the phone rang. It was Norm.

"I thought we might go out earlier than we planned," he said, "if that's okay. Then we can have an early dinner and go to a movie."

"I'm sorry, but I have to break our date. Some food I ate this afternoon made me feel sick." *What a lame excuse.*

"Where did you go?"

"I went to a wedding. Some people I know invited me. Then there was the reception dinner. I got a ride back, and I started to feel sick." Norm seemed content with her explanation, but Merry felt compelled to enhance the explanation. "It was a last-minute invitation from some girls I know."

Apparently, Norm was satisfied with her scant information, for he only told her to feel better and that he'd see her the next day at three thirty.

Merry managed only a faint good-bye.

Twenty-One

November 1973

When Merry woke up the next morning, she dreaded that the tea with Norm's mother was going to be a disaster. She recalled how she'd felt when the invitation first came. Now the same panic swept over her, even though she had already made the decision to stand up Norm and not go to the tea. She was convinced that she had to end her relationship with Norm before she got hurt. She didn't want to hear someone tell her she wasn't good enough.

Her mother's voice rang in her ears. *"That's right, missy. Ya tell 'em yoah on to them and they ahrn't getting any chance to act bettah than ya ahr. But ya should remembah not to try to act as more than ya ahr. See what ya almost got yoahself into? Why can't ya jest be nahmal?"*

It was close to noon, and Merry was still sitting on her bed, worrying. What should she do? The question ran on and on in her mind like a broken record. If she wasn't there when Norm showed up, then he might think something was the matter and wait for her. She couldn't stay out all day. But if she didn't go out at all... Maybe she should call downstairs and tell the receptionist that she wasn't to be disturbed for any reason. Yes, that's what she'd do, and then she'd go back to sleep. She could use a day of just sleeping, though she wanted to take another shower first.

Merry took a long shower and washed her hair. As she stood under the flow of soothing water and closed her eyes, she thought, *If I could stay like this forever...* Her reverie was interrupted when the water started to run cold.

Once back in her room, she looked out the window and saw that it was another gray fall day that threatened to sulk until dark. It was already one thirty. Norm would pick her up in two hours. A net of confusion, doubt, and fear of the uncertain dropped on her with a thud. The phone was right there on her desk, but it might as well have been ten miles away.

Slowly, she reached for the phone and buzzed the reception desk.

"Hi, Rachel. This is Merry. Will you take a message for me?"

Twenty-Two

May 1974

Springtime on Beacon Street was a beautiful sight, with pink-purple blossoms like tiny ballerinas in tutus posing on branches of ornamental crabapple trees. Small patches of green grass sprouted behind the iron gates that protected the large brick and brownstone townhouses. Engraved brass plaques affixed to the facades of the buildings instructed deliverymen and tradesman to use the service entrance. The large front windows glistened in the daylight, allowing passersby a wistful glance at the sun reflecting off a crystal chandelier or a huge fern on a stand placed near the window. It was springtime.

Merry hurried down Boylston Street, carrying a heavy portfolio filled with sketches and fabric samples. She would cut across the Commons on her way to her second appointment on Beacon Street. Reno was now letting her make client calls. In a couple of years, she would finish her course for certification as an interior decorator. She was on her way.

As she passed Shreve, Crump & Low, Norm walked out of the store. "Well, Merry, I haven't seen you for a while." He was gracious—and apparently not angry with her.

She smiled weakly. "It's been a busy winter for me."

"Merry, I'd like you to meet my fiancée, Abby Stoughton."

At first she hadn't seen anyone with Norm. Then she realized the tall young woman with taffy-colored hair and green eyes was with him.

Abby extended a slender hand as she brushed back a stray lock from her flawless pageboy with her other hand. The intention was to show off her diamond engagement ring.

"Hey, good seeing you, Merry. Take care."

"I will." She walked away, thinking that Abby Stoughton was so much better suited for Norm than she would have been. She blinked rapidly against the sudden tears in her eyes. *Must have got some dust in them,* she thought.

What ifs plagued her as she trudged across the Commons. She was too busy with her own thoughts to see the swan boats, feel the sunshine, or exult in the perfect spring day. What if she had answered his calls after she stood him up? She could have told him… what? Nothing. That had been her decision, to say nothing. What if she had gone to meet his mother? It would have been terrible. She had saved herself from being hurt. She'd done the right thing. Hadn't she?

Twenty-Three

June 1981

Seven years quickly passed, and Merry now looked at her work as her life. Nothing else interested her. It was her hobby, her social life, and the only place she felt safe and in charge of herself. At La Viola, she was liked and respected for her talent, her hard work, and her agreeable disposition. For the first time in her life, she was content, because she had created herself in the image she wanted. As the seasons had passed, blurring one into another, she shed the look of insecurity that had once informed others' first impression of her.

She was now twenty-nine years old. The slight girlishness evident in her face even in her mid-twenties had been replaced by the angles and planes of a mature woman, which had sculpted it with a slightly hard look, especially around the mouth. No longer did she squander her money in London Ladies. Time had taught her the refinement of dress, which she emulated from her observations of the elegant clients who patronized La Viola. Merry was now a slender woman who always wore gray or black with touches of white. She wore the same pearl earrings every day. Her hair and nails were done at Elizabeth Arden.

"Dear heart," Reno called, "come into my office when you have the time."

That was his way of saying *right now.* Merry immediately appeared in the doorway.

"Sit down, Merry. Would you like something to drink?
I have a new coffee I'd like you to taste."

She knew Reno didn't ask her into his office just to
drink coffee. "Sounds good to me."

He handed her a cup of the steaming, aromatic
brew. "Good, isn't it?" Before she had the chance to take
one sip, he began to talk. "First of all, congratulations
on getting your interior design certification. I'm going
to open a La Viola in Manhattan in September, and I'll
need someone to manage it for me. Interested?"

Merry almost spilled the coffee. "It would be a chance
of a lifetime for me! What do you want me to do there?"

"First, let me tell you what this is all about. The
Manhattan branch of La Viola will cater mostly to career
women. I want a decorating establishment that women
will use from their first modest apartment to the quan-
tum-jump, big-promotion payoff. La Viola will offer
apartment-sized furniture and feminine fabrics and, at
the same time, keep up with the current trends. And
we will offer our decorating services free and price our
goods from moderate to high. Quality in all cases. I want
you to establish a new client base. I'll give you a list of
prospective clients. Then you are on your own. As of now,
La Viola has twenty families and five corporate clients in
New York."

"When do I start?"

"We'll start with your training tomorrow morning. It
shouldn't be too difficult for you to catch on to, since
you've been doing much of the same work here. The only
thing that will be different is that *you* will keep the sales
records for the Manhattan location. When you get very
busy, you might want to hire a part-time receptionist/
bookkeeper. But that's in the future. The shop will be set

up with fabric samples, furniture, all the essentials, plus an office for you. All the work will be done here in the Boston workroom and shipped to the clients."

"Where will I live? I don't know a thing about New York. In fact, I've never been there."

"So this will be your maiden voyage into the city of tall buildings and high aspirations. I have an apartment not too far from where the shop will be. I've owned it for years but never lived in it. I bought it for investment and rental. The place has the same lumpy furniture that belonged to all the former owners. You can pay a low rent and live at one of the best locations, right by Museum Mile. The apartment is in the back of the building so it has no view, but I suspect you won't be spending a lot of time there."

"What about salary and benefits?"

"A true businesswoman. Same benefits, but you'll get a cost-of-living adjustment to your current salary, which will more than take care of your rent. Or if you like, you can *not* pay rent and keep the same salary. Rest assured, Merry, there will be increases as we establish and grow the business in the city."

"I'm practically packed."

"It will be a good experience for you, although I'll be losing my best assistant. Why don't you finish your coffee? Now, you won't spill it."

By summer's end, before late August's first surprise chilly day, Merry was a certified member of the National Society of Interior Decorators. The day the certificate arrived, Reno had held an impromptu after-work celebration party. Wine, hors d'oeuvres, and piles of fresh shrimp were served in his large living-room–style office. When it was over, Merry walked back to the Standish. The sun had set, and the walk to her room was a dreary, lonely trek past closed office buildings, across a small bridge and a vacant lot. Finally, a dull light midway down the block signaled she was at the Standish. Not once did she ever think of the place as home. Rather, she often reflected that she was the official old maid of the Standish.

A stack of "homework" now sat on her desk. It was information she needed to work in New York. As far as Merry was concerned, she was already out of Boston. She sat at her desk to work, and when she finally looked at her clock, it was past midnight. She'd forgotten to eat dinner, but thanks to Reno's lavish spread, she wasn't hungry. Half an hour later, she was sound asleep.

The next day, Reno called her into his office again. For the last couple of months, they had been working as teacher and pupil. Merry had been learning the business side of La Viola and, surprising herself, she grasped everything quickly and was enjoying what she was learning.

"That's enough for today," Reno finally said a few hours later. "Any questions?"

"Not that I can think of at the moment."

"Fine. Then how about giving me an answer to this question: Will you join me after work for a drink?"

"Any special reason?"

"It's my forty-first birthday, and I'm still an old maid. I thought we might have dinner afterward and continue our discussions about New York."

"Happy birthday, Reno! And if anyone is going to end up an old maid, it will be me."

"Then we'll console each other while we get some work done. I was thinking Joseph's."

Merry had all but forgotten about the first and last time she had been there. It seemed like a hundred years ago. "Sounds good. Will we leave right after work?"

"No, you go home and make yourself even more beautiful. I'll pick you up at seven. But mind you—this is not a date!"

"A date? Reno, you're my boss." She smiled. "How can it be a date?"

"Clever girl. At seven, then."

Back at the Standish, Merry thought about the girl she had once been—the fearful little girl who didn't think anything would ever happen in her life. Now she was going out to one of Boston's finest restaurants with her elegant, successful boss. And soon she would be managing a decorating store in New York. Merry could imagine her mother's comment: *"Ahrn't you the one. All fancy mannuhs."*

Merry hurled back an imaginary response. *Thank you for sharing your observation.* Then she took a quick shower, changed, and was waiting in the lobby just before seven.

Reno created quite a stir when he entered the lobby. A little over six feet tall, with prematurely silver-gray hair, a broad dimpled smile, and flashing brown eyes, he caused the women to buzz, "Who is this guy?" and "What's a good-looking guy doing in a joint like this?"

Merry walked over to Reno, who gave her a friendly hug. Some of the women pretended to swoon. Refinement wasn't exactly a requisite for living at the Standish.

Twenty-Four

E arly the next month, Merry was packed and ready to head for her new adventure. Reno was going with her. He would help her move into her new apartment over the weekend and show her around the new Second Avenue La Viola. In two weeks, the studio would be open for business.

Reno had hired a limousine and driver so he and Merry could spend the time working and finalizing what they needed to do over the next two days. It was a great feeling to be thought of as a necessary person, someone who mattered. The drive to the city seemed to be over before it started. The limousine pulled up to an imposing white-stone apartment house on the Upper East Side. A uniformed doorman opened the car door and helped Merry to the sidewalk. *If this isn't real,* she thought, *then I've really gone insane.*

"This is it," Reno said. "Let's go up and see the damage."

He guided her to the elevator while the doorman and chauffeur dealt with her belongings. When they reached the sixth floor, they got out and walked down a brightly lit hall to a door at the end. Reno handed the key to Merry.

"Your first apartment, dear heart."

The door opened to a somewhat shabbily furnished apartment that faced the back of the building and over-looked a small inner courtyard.

"What do you think?"

"It's wonderful, Reno. I love it. This is my first real home since…" Her voice trailed off.

"If you're going to get all gushy, you'll make my mascara run."

"Reno, you don't wear—"

"I know, but some of my clients get a kick out of that kind of talk. I'd better watch out before it becomes second nature. So, let's have a glass of wine to welcome you to a new beginning." He opened a leather briefcase he'd brought in with him and produced a bottle of wine, two glasses, and a small box of cheese and crackers.

"You thought of everything," Merry said. "Once I find the kitchen, I'll see if there's a corkscrew."

"I have one. Once a boy scout, always… um… be prepared or something."

They opened the windows in the apartment. All four of them. One in the living room, one in the bedroom, one in the tiny bathroom, and—the prize of all city apart-ments—a window in the kitchen.

"I wouldn't spend too much money on this place, dear heart. Wait until you can get some really good samples from our vendors."

Reno sat down on the living room sofa and opened the bottle of wine. "To you, Merry, and the new La Viola."

She took her glass and touched it to Reno's. There was nothing else to say. She was too happy and eager to start her new life.

Reno broke the comfortable silence. "Merry, don't hesitate to call me if you need me. Even if you just want to talk. I told you once that you could always talk to me, and I still mean it. Although I don't recall your ever coming to me with any problems, work-related or not. Just keep that in mind." They heard thumping out in the hall. "Must be your things arriving. You probably want to get settled. I'll pick you up around—"

"Seven?" she cut in.

"She's so smart. Seven." He kissed her on the forehead. "That's for good luck."

"Seven," Merry said again. Reno smiled and left as the doorman and driver carried her few possessions into the apartment.

Late Sunday afternoon, Reno had returned to Boston, and Merry was alone on her much-used sofa in her first real home—a place that was quiet, comfortable, and best of all, just for her. Even the shabby furniture appealed to Merry. It looked homey, lived-in—not like a showroom but a place where she could be happy.

Happy, she thought. *That's a word I haven't had much to do with.*

But there she was, happy, all wrapped up in her little cocoon. And when she emerged from this safe place, she'd feel like a beautiful butterfly. But this butterfly was getting hungry, so she'd better go out and see what she could find.

She laughed at herself. As if there were no restaurants or grocery stores around the corner. This was New York City. If she wanted a fried yak sandwich, she could find a place that served it. They'd probably even ask if she'd like a side of boiled hoofs with it.

Out on the street, Merry walked a short block to Madison Avenue, a street of dreams waiting to become real. Antique shops, jewelers, dress shops, stationers, a myriad of discreet restaurants. Stands of ripe fruits and bouquets of bright flowers lingered seductively in front of a tiny grocery store, luring the curious and the hungry into its small den of gastronomic delights. Merry stopped and selected a bunch of bright orange lilies, some grapes, and some pears. Once inside, the amazing array of takeout foods, with their enticing aromas, drew her to a huge glass case that held the makings of a very good evening meal.

I even have my own grocery store, she thought. *Now all I need is my own boyfriend.*

Her reverie was suddenly interrupted.

"Merry?" A man's voice came from behind her. Merry turned around to see an attractive man in corduroys and cashmere smiling at her. "Don't you remember me?" he said. "Randy Grant from the architectural firm in Boston? You brought samples to our office."

"Randy. Of course. But that was ages ago. What are you doing here in the city?" She was careful to use the new language she'd picked up from magazines: the city for Manhattan; Apollinaris for sparkling water; Brie or Bel Paese for fine cheese; Bloomie's for the iconic department store.

"Never forget a face," Randy said. "I live here now, working at our New York office. You?"

"I work here too. I'm managing La Viola's new Second Avenue decorating studio."

"When did this happen?"

"I got here this weekend. The studio opens in two weeks."

"Be sure to invite me to the opening. I'm in the book. R. A. Grant."

"I won't forget."

Merry carried her purchases back to her apartment. She was pleased that she looked like any other city denizen, carrying a bag of groceries and that bunch of glorious orange lilies.

Twenty-Five

January 1995

Caressed by the chiffon-like Palm Beach breeze that danced around her shoulders, Merry walked across the street from her hotel and one block down for her three o'clock appointment at Salon Martine.

On Saturdays, the place was a hive of activity. All the manicure stations were filled. Cans of hairspray were waved over clients' heads with the virtuosity of batons being wielded by concert maestros.

Merry was greeted by a cordial but preoccupied receptionist who was answering the ever-ringing phone, receiving payment for services, while attempting to re-attach one of her false eyelashes.

"You're Mr. Martine's three o'clock." With an index fingernail as long as a tongue depressor, she hit a button on the phone and announced, "Marty. Your three o'clock."

Mr. Martine, né Marty Gruzkovich, emerged from the back of the salon, making an entrance worthy of a dinner theater emcee.

"You are fortunate I had the time free," he told Merry. "My standing three o'clock had an unexpected funeral. Hers. My chair is over there." He pointed to a private booth that connoted his status as an artiste.

Merry took a seat in the surprisingly comfortable salon chair.

"Let's see what we're working with." Mr. Martine fingered her hair as if he were a forensic detective looking for crime clues. "A lot of dead ends. Dry body. What you need is a good moisturizing and a blow job."

Tell me about it. "Whatever it takes," she said.

"Don't worry, sweetie. I've seen worse than this. At least you're not over-processed. You could scrub a pot with the wiry hair we see from over-bleaching. So let's get you washed. Maria, sink number *tres!* And let her sit for *cinco minutos* with her moisturizer."

Maria took fifteen minutes to wash and moisturize. It felt great. Merry would have been content to lie back and be pampered for another hour.

When she was back in the styling chair, Mr. Martine took another look at the crime scene. "You really should trim those blunt ends. And I think... yes, a highlighting. You're too attractive to wear such a—how can I say it, sweetie?—such a drab color. It definitely is not Palm Beach."

"Let's go for it."

"You'll be here for a while. Champagne or Chablis?"

"The color or the drink?"

"Both. A couple of champagnes, and you'll be ready for anything. But with three, you'll be relaxed enough for a full body wax."

"I'll have one glass, please."

Mr. Martine snapped on his latex gloves with the gravity of a surgeon about to separate conjoined twins. After all, basic color and highlighting were two separate procedures.

Merry closed her eyes. She actually was relaxed. This could get to be a habit—an expensive one. Her thoughts were interrupted by a conversation at the manicure table outside her booth.

"I finally got Mon Sewer Mawk to do me. I had to wait three months."

"I hear he does all the big ones in Pawm Beach. Everybody wants him to do them. An old lady over at the Biltmore swears by him. He's been over there at least five times."

"It's really tough to get someone who knows how to do good fawking. My girlfriend said he fawked ha purple in ha bedroom, and it came out just drop dead. Then ha husband wanted to do it in his owfice."

From the accents, Merry deduced both the manicurist and the client were from Long Island. She further deduced that the walls of their homes were being painted by Monsieur Mark, the faux paint artist.

She dozed off, thinking, *I always wondered how to use "faux" as a verb.*

She woke when the timer bell went off, and Mr. Martine raked his fingers through her hair, checking the color distribution.

"Perfect. I just love it. Maria, sink *tres*."

The washing process was repeated. It was only another fifteen minutes, but Merry felt as if it was taking forever. She wanted to see her new color. Colors.

Back to Mr. Martine. Clip. Snip. Shape. Drape.

Out came the blow dryer. Slowly, he twirled his brush through her new Palm Beach mane. As her hair dried, she could see warm golden strands blending with the strands of sun-kissed hair that framed her face.

"Sweetie, you're a knockout."

"I can't believe it. This looks great. My hair never looked so good."

"Didn't I tell you?" he said.

As if the final act of a play was over, Mr. Martine whipped the styling cape from her shoulders. "Okay, sweetie, you can see Doreen at the desk." Pressing his intercom, he asked, "Is my five o'clock comb-out here?"

The calm produced by the champagne and pampering came to an abrupt halt when Doreen, the receptionist, presented the bill to Merry. *My God, I could almost fly to Paris on this.*

"Is everything all right?" Doreen asked.

"Yes. I'll write you a check."

Doreen shrugged. "Cash. Check. Credit card." She was preoccupied with regluing another detached eyelash.

"That's two hundred fifty dollars, right?" Merry said, just to make sure there wasn't a mistake.

"Plus tips. Mr. Martine always gets twenty percent, and the shampoo girl gets five dollars per sink trip."

"Of course."

Merry wrote out a check for the full amount. Doreen gave her cash back for the tips, telling her that the tip envelopes were next to the candy dish. Merry dutifully stuffed the folded bills into little perfumed envelopes. She handed one to the sink girl and slipped Mr. Martine's onto his counter. He barely nodded in acknowledgement, and she was sure the sink girl would forget her as soon as she walked out.

It was five thirty. After that experience, Merry found she wasn't the least bit hungry.

Twenty-Six

January 1995

When Merry returned to the hotel, no one was at the front desk. There was no one in the bar or sitting around the pool. *Everyone is somewhere, and I'm in a perpetual here. Alone.*

She soothed her thoughts by promising herself another great soak in the swan tub. *If I spend any more time in that tub, I'm going to look like a prune with a two hundred and fifty dollar, plus tips, color job. Maybe I shouldn't put any water in the tub—just sit there and read. That way, the steam won't ruin my... will you stop obsessing about this? When was the last time you had your hair done? Aren't you worth anything to yourself? Oh, shut up and run the water.*

Merry was a pro at making herself miserable.

She was just getting out of the tub when the phone rang. Who would call her here? Randy's office? She felt a surge of excitement.

It was a man but not Randy. He introduced himself as Barry Chadwick, the general contractor who was building Randy's house. Merry confirmed that Randy's receptionist, Sally, had told her he would be picking her up at nine on Monday to take her to the worksite. He suggested instead that he take her to brunch the next day, and they could go to the site after that. Would eleven o'clock work for her? She said it sounded fine. She'd be in the lobby at eleven.

All of a sudden, Merry felt hungry. Next to the post office, she recalled, was a luncheonette with an old-fashioned eight-stool counter and four small tables. The neon sign in the window announced, "Open from Seven to Midnight. Breakfast All Day." The Ocean Breeze Luncheonette, known to the locals as Breezy's, would be perfect.

Diners at Breezy's lunch counter were not there because of its ambiance. It was cheap. The regulars assembled there every night when they got off their private nursing shifts or after conducting hour-long aerobics classes to chubby matrons at the Chateau Celeste by the Sea. An off-duty chauffeur read the newspaper while his employers were across the street dining on French cuisine at Les Trois Amis.

Merry sat at the counter. A waitress swabbed the area in front of her and slapped the menu down.

"Coffee now or with your order?"

"Now, please."

The waitress brought the coffee. "The hot meatloaf sandwich is good. It's fresh."

That kind of a pronouncement was something Merry had been hoping not to hear. *Perhaps,* she thought, *I should inquire what's stale.* She ordered an English muffin.

"That's all? The soup's homemade."

"Just the coffee and muffin, for now."

"The key lime pie's a favorite."

Merry patted her midriff. "Dieting."

The waitress slapped the check down on the counter and then patted her ample hip. "Tell me about it." She pivoted to the next customer. "Mrs. Gorman, how was the cruise? Your usual takeout? Coconut cake too? You're going to spoil your girlish figure, Mrs. Gorman."

"Viv, honey, I'm eighty-two years old. I'll live danger-ously. If I'm lucky, I'll live long enough to get back to the apartment to eat it. Put on some of that chocolate sauce. And don't be stingy."

Merry sipped the coffee, which had a slightly bitter taste. The English muffin, covered with overly sweet marmalade, somewhat hid the taste of the coffee. Twenty-five minutes later, she was back at the hotel. The night clerk was there, engrossed in a Harley-Davidson brochure. Unnoticed, Merry went upstairs. She was asleep the minute her head hit the pillow.

Twenty-Seven

January 1995

Another sunny Palm Beach morning. Palm Beach, that narrow barrier island, lovingly referred to as Fantasy Island. Unlike a mythical fantasy island, here wishes might come true. The lore of unimaginable wealth is fueled by the dreams of those caught on the bottom edge of the wheel of fortune.

Merry awoke refreshed. Her morning coffee and the Sunday paper were on the way. Sunshine danced through the windows and beckoned her to look outside at the brilliant fuchsia bougainvillea that draped itself over the roof of the gazebo at the corner of the patio. The tops of the palm trees swayed in graceful rhythm to the wind blowing in from the ocean. A fountain spouted water into the air, and sunlit rainbow colors splashed into the pool. The turquoise water of the crescent-shaped swimming pool glistened under the early morning sun. Puffy white clouds in stately leisure floated across the clear blue sky. Everything was silent. She could have been looking at an Impressionist painting—only this was real.

The local Sunday paper was accompanied by "Cotillions and Cocktails," a glossy, glitzy international tabloid with offices in Milan and Zurich. The January issue featured social life on the island. That social life was primarily the fund-raising efforts of benefactors who endowed hospitals, cultural centers, museums, operas, and ballet companies. Hospitals and disease-of-the-month galas were always oversubscribed.

The women's auxiliaries of these events were photographed in the lush Mediterranean-style gardens of the chairwomen's homes. One current chairwoman had held the position for thirty-five years. Most of the women in the pictures were of indeterminate age, and they all looked the same. Somewhere between forty and forty-one, blonde, trim, porcelain smiles glinting in the sunlight. Some were Princess this or Countess that. There were Dee Dees and Cee Cees, hyphenated last names, and many Mrs. So-and-So the Third or Fourth. Merry wondered if that meant the wife's marital status or the husband's family name.

Advertisements in the magazine discreetly offered diamonds from ten to twenty carats. In small print was, "Larger stones on request." There were offerings for yachts and Rolls-Royces. Advertisements informed prospective clients of the availability of seasonal rentals at $25,000 a month, four months minimum. Full-page ads hawked yet-to-be-built luxury condominiums, starting at preconstruction prices of three million, and proclaimed that 80 percent were already sold. Medium-sized ads usually were taken by cosmetic dentists and plastic surgeons. Those ads featured models with vacant expressions, as if posed by a taxidermist.

Merry was used to reading the society news, but this, she mused, was somewhere between a comic book and a hallucination.

Merry had yet to learn the social geography of this island paradise, whose map resembled a magnificent Aubusson carpet with its central pattern, surrounding color field, borders, and fringe. In the center resided the generous, rarely seen megawealthy. The color field contained the generous, occasionally seen super-wealthy. The border designs defined the private clubs, interest groups, and charities. The fringe was for those who hoped for access by volunteering on committees and buying tickets to the myriad charity events. And as with any carpet, constant use generated lint—those who were beyond the fringe.

Merry was in the lobby by eleven. Three couples were at the registration desk, getting directions to Singer Island. The receptionist smiled at Merry.

Within two minutes, a maroon Rolls-Royce Silver Shadow appeared under the porte cochère. The bellman opened the car door with a greeting that always assured a generous tip.

And Barry Chadwick was a big tipper. It was as much his trademark to those who provided menial services as was his generous gift-giving to plumbing and electrical contractors. The cement and marble contractors were all on a first-name basis with him. Mr. Barry Chadwick also was a big favorite with local zoning boards. To his office and housekeeping staff, he was affectionately known as the Baron. Once you were hired by Chadwick, Inc., you had a job for life—if you didn't screw up. Everyone got the same treatment. One chance.

Barry Chadwick strode into the lobby as if he owned the place. In actuality, he was only a one-quarter owner.

"You must be Merry Venture."

"The same. I'm looking forward to seeing the site."

"I have a brunch reservation at The Breakers. Been there?"

"This is my first time in Palm Beach."

"Great. Let's go." Barry did not waste words.

When the Silver Shadow pulled up to The Breakers, a parking valet took the keys and joined the procession of other Rolls to the parking area. Of course, there were Bentleys and Jaguars too. Merry wondered if people driving cars in need of washing had to park a couple of blocks away.

The Breakers lobby swirled with Sunday-morning activity. People were checking in and out. A bridal party stood at the far end, waiting for the photographer to pose them for immortality. Suntanned couples in golf attire lounged on deep sofas. People who looked familiar because they were famous nodded to gaunt young women and muscular men in trendy garb and sunglasses and speaking Italian. Weary parents dragged a screaming child out the door.

Barry guided Merry into the vast dining room. The maître d' greeted Barry, looked at Merry, and gave a sign of approval with a subtle flutter of the eye. He led them to a table with a view of the ocean.

The dining room was enormous, yet for all its gargantuan size, it was warm and inviting. The soothing decor—high ceiling, deep carpet, and draperies—muffled conversations so they were no more obtrusive than the crash of the ocean against the shore. The waiter, noting that Merry was wearing black slacks, quickly exchanged the white napkin for a black one and spread it on her lap.

"Not too early for champagne for you, is it?" Barry asked.

"No. But a glass of orange juice would be nice too."

The attentive waiter placed a full pitcher of orange juice on the table. A corps de ballet could not have been more precise, graceful, or noiseless than the staff was in executing its service.

Barry motioned for Merry to join him at the sumptuous buffet tables. Merry was no stranger to buffets. Often, she would treat a client to the Sunday buffet at the Plaza Athénée, which was considered by many to be one of the best in New York. She couldn't help but compare the sight that stood before her to that at the Athénée: long-skirted buffet tables with food arranged in patterns as intricate as an ancient Italian mosaic. Most impressive were the fruits laid out like paintings in the style of the Renaissance painter Arcimboldo, who portrayed human busts made out of various fruits and vegetables. However, the chief food stylist of The Breakers' buffet also felt it best to interpret this style with palm trees, golf courses, and dolphins. Merry later found out that during the holidays, The Breakers would have a Christmas tree fashioned of limes, avocados, and green grapes, and garlanded by clusters of red grapes, lemons, oranges, kumquats, and unshelled nuts. A fresh display was made up each weekend from Thanksgiving to Christmas Day.

She served herself a shelled lobster tail, shirred eggs, and fresh asparagus.

"You're a small eater," Barry said.

"Compared to what's here, yes."

The waiter placed an ice-filled champagne bucket next to Barry and held out the bottle for Barry's approval. Barry filled the glasses and offered a toast.

"Here's to a successful working relationship. I take it you've known Randy for a long time."

"Since the days when we were in Boston. A long time."

From then on, the conversation between them consisted of silence interspersed with comments regarding the excellent buffet, the magnificent ocean view, and the great service. But the silent stretches weren't awkward. Not for Merry, since by nature her guard was always up, and Barry seemed comfortable with a minimum of conversation.

After they had finished the more-than-satisfying brunch, he looked at his watch. "Getting on to one. Let's go to the site."

The ride down South Ocean Boulevard was spectacular. Moorish castles, Mediterranean villas, and homes of movie stars, communications magnates, and class-action attorneys loomed up like pastel-painted sunbathers on the beach. Great palm trees lined the gated driveways. Still to be completed, Barry pointed out to her, was a fifty-room, twenty-two bath compound for some Mideast oil potentate.

At last, they reached the site of the home of the future Mr. and Mrs. Randy Grant. Even though the selection of plumbing fixtures, tiles, and kitchen appliances still needed to be added to the mansion, the completely land-scaped property foretold the picture of an overwhelming estate, with its commanding and unobstructed view of the ocean. Great windows in the front and back of the house opened onto balconies that invited a constant cross breeze from the trade winds. A loggia swept around the first floor in an undulating series of curves. There were a dozen rooms, Merry knew. It was certainly not as big as the other mansions but far more graceful—and it cost only seven million, according to Barry.

Seven million dollars. Merry couldn't wait to see the inside of seven million. As they walked through the loggia, she mused, *It could have been me… if I wasn't so… oh, give it a rest.*

"What do you think?" Barry asked, as he unrolled a series of plans on a worktable.

"I'll need to see the rest of the place."

"Come on." He took two hardhats off the worktable. Giving one to Merry, he strode through the foyer as if he were the only one there.

Merry followed, thinking that for all his obvious wealth, Barry apparently had a vocabulary of fifty words.

The stairway of polished, pale travertine marble curved like a satin ribbon, floating upward. Overhead, an oval window invited the sun to melt the stairs into a flow of rich cream. Merry fancied it could be the stairway to paradise.

For the next hour, she was introduced to the almost-completed house. She made notes and wiped dust out of her eyes as Barry pointed out the areas that still needed finishing and their projected completion dates.

"That's it for now," he said at last. "Any questions?"

"Not right now."

"You'll need a car. Did you rent one?"

"I was going to do that tomorrow morning."

"Don't bother. You can drive one of the company cars. I'll send one this afternoon."

"That's very nice of you. Thanks."

Barry disabused her of thinking this was something special. "We always provide a car for our decorators. Part of our operating expenses."

"Well, thanks anyway."

"No problem. The plumbing contractor's coming at seven tomorrow morning, but you can be here at nine. You can talk about the fixtures with him then." Barry looked at his Rolex. "It's three o'clock. Want some lunch?"

"Not after that big brunch. But I *am* thirsty after all this dust."

"We can have something to drink over at the Four Seasons. Let's go."

What gives with this guy? Merry thought. *He talks like a robot and has the personality of a tree.* She followed him out to the car.

The mansions of South Ocean Boulevard disappeared at Sloan's Curve, and the condominium and hotel area began. Sparkling oceanfront buildings protected by security guards in station houses and doormen lined the eastern side of the road. Since it was January and early in the season, many of the apartment windows were still covered with storm shutters. These were the million-dollar seasonal retreats. Farther down, on the west side of the road, condos and co-ops faced west to the inter-coastal waterway. Everyone enjoyed the same sunshine, saw the same tropical birds flying overhead, and were seduced by the same tropical breezes.

Discreetly placed away from the road and behind a park-sized expanse of driveway loomed the Four Seasons Hotel, a Taj Mahal of elegance. Barry's Rolls sauntered up the drive as if on automatic pilot and heading for home. Two valets jumped to attention to open the car doors and take the keys. They both flashed the usual pre-thank-you tip smiles.

"We'll sit outside on the patio," Barry said. "The ocean view's great."

The broad marble lobby led to the tented patio area. At the wrought-iron umbrella tables sat lean, vibrant young men and women who had the look of the aggressively successful—custom sunglasses and beautiful golden tans. Long-legged women had flung their Gucci, Hermès, Vuitton, and Chanel bags over their chair backs. Mingled with laughter, the cadences of French, Italian, and German bounced from table to table like ping-pong balls.

The maître d' immediately greeted them. "Mr. Chadwick, nice to see you. When did you get back from the Europe?"

Georges knew his regulars and where they liked to sit, and he personally delivered each client's drink of choice.

No need to ask. Georges kept a mental file when it came to who was who—and who wasn't. It was his job.

A waiter arrived with iced teas as soon as they sat down. The only sound at their table was the ice melting in the frosted glasses.

"So now that you've seen it, what do you think of Randy's place?" Barry asked, though he seemed distracted.

"It's a challenge. Has he been down here much?"

"Just once. To buy the property."

"Oh." She watched the ice dissolve in her now-sweating glass, trying to think of something to continue the conversation. "How do you know him?"

"School. MIT. I was a year ahead of him. He was architecture; I was mechanical engineering. Randy was lots of fun."

She thought that might have been the longest string of words he had uttered all day.

"What else have you done for him?" she asked.

"Nothing down here, but my construction company has done shopping malls and residential stuff all over the Northeast." A long pause as he drank his iced tea. "You?"

"Me, what?"

"What have you done for him?"

"This is my first job with Randy. I've known him for years, as a friend."

"And now?"

"He thinks my decorating style will be what his future wife will like. According to Randy, she wants to leave it all up to me. Odd, but that's how it is."

"The soft-shell crabs are good here. Want some?"

"Um... all right."

Barry caught the waiter's attention. "Bryan, a couple of soft-shell crabs. And a couple of Chardonnays." He turned back to Merry. "Then you know something about Elizabeth."

Once again, that sinking feeling hit the pit of Merry's stomach. Reality had set in with the end of foolish dreaming. No more foolish hopes. Randy was finally gone forever.

"English," she answered. "Lives in a stately English manor house and has no interest or idea about furnishing. I guess she was born furnished."

"I understand the estate has been in the family for generations," Barry added.

What a scintillating conversationalist, Merry thought as she toyed with what was left of the iced tea. They consumed the crabs and drank the wine with no comments other than "Delicious" or "The best."

Once again, Barry consulted his watch. "Four thirty. Want anything else?"

"No, this was fine. Just right."

"Good." He stood up, signaling the end of the meeting.

The waiter pulled the chair out for Merry. Barry placed two crisp hundred-dollar bills on the table. Merry could only surmise one was for the bill and the other was a tip for Bryan. On the way out, Barry shook Georges's hand, into which he deposited another hundred dollars.

As they approached the door, the Silver Shadow pulled up and the valets opened the doors. Barry handed each one a ten-dollar bill.

"You like music?" He turned on the tape deck before she had a chance to answer. They were back at her hotel in ten minutes.

A gray Jaguar and a driver were waiting in the driveway. "That's your car, Merry. Nine o'clock tomorrow." He called to the Jaguar's driver, "Luis, come on in with me.

I'll drop you off." The driver got into the front seat of the Shadow, and they were gone.

Merry walked into the hotel lobby.

"Do you want me to park your car in your spot, Miss Venture?" The bellman looked only too eager to get behind the wheel of that baby.

"Yes. Please." She produced a five-dollar bill.

Welcome to Palm Beach, she thought as she stepped into the opened elevator. It wasn't five o'clock, but for her, the day was over.

Twenty-Eight

January 1995

There's nothing like a good night's sleep and an early-morning Jaguar, Merry thought the next day. *I could get very used to this. But if you're smart, and I know you are, you'll just get the job done and leave the mansion dreams alone. Well,* she told herself, *thank you for sharing.*

When she arrived, the site was filled with construction workers. Dust swirled. The noise of hammering and drilling surrounded what clearly was the plumbing contractor. He had that I'm-in-charge look. His printed T-shirt read DeStefano Plumbing and Heating. The T-shirt emphasized the fact that its wearer was built like a weightlifter.

His greeting acknowledged he was expecting her. "Noisy, huh? Tony DeStefano. You must be Merry Venture." Tony held out a hand big enough to pick up a bathtub. "Seen the place yet?"

Taking the giant appendage, Merry said that she had been there on Sunday with Barry.

"We've got some tile samples here. All imported from Italy. DeStefano does marble, tile, plumbing, and electrical. Hey, Gino, can you keep it down a minute? I can't hear myself think!" The hammering stopped, but the drilling didn't.

With Randy's luck, they'll probably strike oil. Merry smiled at the thought.

"I got samples on the loggia," Tony added.

Merry followed along to the back of the house, where there were at least a hundred sample boards of tile colors and designs. It looked like a tomb excavation.

"We want to get the tile in by early next month," Tony said. "Think there'll be a problem?"

"Not with all these choices. The first thing I want to do is create some sketches with color selections. I'll have to see the fixtures too."

"No problem. Everything else is at the showroom. I'm going there now. If you don't mind riding in a truck, we could go now. You can work with Gina. She's good."

Merry climbed into the truck, which was surprisingly neat and dust-free.

As they drove, Tony pointed to several mansions where his contracting firm had worked. "Some of these places have ten or more bathrooms. We just finished a place. The owner wanted the decorator to put in tiles that didn't do a thing for the baths. All ten of them. The decorator told her it would look like crap—in nicer language—but the owner insisted that was what she wanted. She decided all this from pictures she saw in magazines. When the client finally came down to inspect the place, she calmly said—and this is after spending twenty grand for each bathroom tile job—'This is dreadful. Pull it out and do something else.' So we did just that, and she was happy."

Merry wondered if this was meant to be a cautionary tale or just coming from the contractor's storytelling ability.

"See that place over there?" Tony went on. "We did that job too. Everything's electronic. The guy has everything remote. Lights, plumbing, you name it. Even the damn toilets flush by remote. Only the best. Money is no object. But try collecting the bill. When our book-keeper calls him, even she's put on remote. And we're still waiting."

"So what do you plan to do?"

"Every time I go past his house, I use my master remote and all his toilets flush, the showers go on, and the pool drains. Watch this." Tony pressed a button on a remote, and the lawn sprinklers sprouted and sprayed.

Twenty-Nine

January 1995

By late afternoon, Merry was satisfied with her selections at the showroom. Gina loaded them into a van and dropped Merry and the samples back at the site and then helped Merry transfer the samples to her car. When Merry returned to the hotel, dinner was the furthest thing from her mind. Around three o'clock, Gina— who was Tony's one-woman office staff—had ordered two pizzas, in case anyone got hungry. Gina ate almost an entire large pizza herself as she talked on the phone, greeted customers, answered questions for Merry, and, from time to time, dabbed splashes of nail polish on her long acrylic nails to see if she liked the shade. Gina was Tony's sister's daughter. Everyone who worked at DeStefano's was related. They were as tight with one another as the cement they used to set tile and marble.

Merry was eager to start her sketches. Which made her wonder about Elizabeth. How could anyone be so uninterested in a house that was being built for her? How could she not want to have some input, even a color preference? Maybe she's blind.

That Randy had told her to use her judgment and finish the project to her taste seemed so uncharacteristic of him. He always knew just how things should be. Even if his fiancée wasn't interested, why wasn't he? Maybe that's what love did to a guy. *Miss Venture, will you please mind your own business and start the damned sketches?*

Merry worked without stop until almost midnight. After a cool bath, she was careful to wrap her hair in a scarf so it would stay looking fresh. After all, she was now one of those Jaguar blondes.

The sound of the ringing telephone blasted her from a wonderful floating sleep. Her travel clock showed 8:00 a.m.

"Yes?" She was still too sleepy to sound coherent.

"Merry? Caprice. Your service told me where you I could get you."

"Cappy, is this important? Or could it wait until I've had my coffee?"

"Listen to this. On Saturday, Tyler and I were at Tiffany. He wants me to have an engagement ring. We're already married, for God's sake."

"This is what you called to tell me at eight in the morning?"

"There's more. Guess who we bumped into at the diamond counter?"

"I haven't the slightest idea."

"Guess."

"The Sultan of Brunei? I don't know."

"Randy, that's who. Wanna know what happened?"

"Should I say no?"

"Randy wasn't alone. He was with some woman, and they were picking out engagement rings. And they weren't puny ones either."

"Were you standing there with a loupe?"

"Merry, you poor thing. He's going to get married."

"I know. That's why I'm down here. I'm decorating his house—all twelve rooms, plus a lanai, a loggia, and a solarium."

"I knew he was well-off, but a house in Palm Beach! I'm sorry, Merry. It should have been you."

"No, it shouldn't. It wasn't that kind of a thing. We were, and still are, friends. The only thing that's changed is that I'm decorating the house for Randy and his fiancée. I'll be working here until April."

"Lots of cute guys down there. Met anyone yet?"

"Cappy, I don't have your talent for meeting, marrying, and burying. I'm down here to work, not to trawl."

"Suit yourself. But it doesn't hurt to keep a sharp eye out."

"I'll have that embroidered on one of the pillows for my spring line."

"I just got a new column at *Zee Zee*. I'm doing a food column."

"When did all this happen?"

"When we got back from Las Vegas. I'm calling it 'Fruits and Tarts.'"

"But you don't know anything about cooking. Whose recipes are you planning to use?"

"No, it's a *Zee Zee* column. You know, 'Breakfast In Bed or How to Do It Sunny-Side Up.' 'One Hundred Ways to Stuff a Potato.' 'Whipped Cream for Beginners.' The best one is, 'How to Make Him a Real Thanksgiving Dinner.'"

"Are you serious?"

"Oh, yeah. I showed a draft to the editorial department, and if we get a good response, we'll spin it out as a paperback."

"Great. Wonderful. I'll call you later on this week."

"You aren't mad that I told you about Randy?"

"I'll send you a thank-you note."

Talking with Caprice is always fun, Merry thought as she got out of bed. She seemed like a nutcase, but she was as straight as a guided missile. She'd have to send Cappy a wedding present. She just hoped the marriage lasted long enough for the package to arrive.

Thirty

January 1995

Merry had no weekend plan. She decided to have her hair done, get a manicure, and sit around the pool with a good book. The hotel bookshelf had some light reading. After checking with her message service and calling Bloomie's to have a silver picture frame sent to Caprice as a wedding gift, she made a Saturday morning appointment at Salon Martine. *What the heck?* she thought, and made it a standing appointment for a wash and blow dry. *When in Palm Beach...*

Merry put some notes together for the following week. She would be looking for furniture, fabrics, and accessories on Antique Row in West Palm. Before she left New York, she had compiled a list of dealers who were likely to have everything she might need. She would make her appointments on Monday. As she was about to head over to Martine's, the phone rang. It was Barry, asking if she was doing anything that weekend.

"I haven't planned much," she answered.

"I'm going out to my boat. How about joining me?"

"When? And where is this boat?"

"This afternoon. The boat's in Nassau. We'll fly down. My friend's lending me his plane."

"Thank you, but I don't think so."

"Why not? Are you afraid of flying?"

"Of course not. Barry, I don't know you. I appreciate the invitation, but no."

"Then how about lunch? You know me well enough to join me for lunch."

"All right, lunch. And please don't say in Paris."

"No, I'll cancel Nassau. I meant someplace around here. Bice is good."

"Fine. About one?"

"I'll pick you up."

Nassau? What the hell was that all about? The guy must be crazy. Going to lunch was one thing, but flying to Nassau? She'd had one business meeting with him. This was business, and she intended to keep it that way. Nassau?

Merry locked the door to her suite and walked over to Salon Martine.

After forty minutes at the salon, Merry walked over to Saks and bought a pair of silk slacks, a linen shirt, a pair of sandals, and a straw hat. By the time she got back to her suite, she had twenty minutes to get ready for lunch. She took a quick bath, freshened her makeup, and dove into her new clothes. She fluffed out her hair and applied a quick spray of Salon Martine's special formula. And finished.

When she exited the elevator, she found Barry waiting. Her first thought was how good-looking he was—tall, tanned, and built like an Olympic tennis player. But what would they talk about?

A different chauffeur opened the rear passenger door to a gray Aston Martin. Merry wanted to quip, "What happened? Lose your license?" but she thought better of it.

"I don't want to drive today," Barry said. "Luis is going to take Mildred for a bath."

"Mildred?"

"The car. So Carl is filling in for today."

They got out at Bice, where the maître d' made the usual fuss. "Mr. Chadwick, how nice to see you. I have your usual table. Ramon will bring the wine."

Ramon appeared and presented a bottle for Barry's approval. Barry said, "Looks good. Has Angela had the baby yet?"

"Last Thursday, Mr. Chadwick. A girl." Ramon poured a bit of wine for Barry to taste.

"Nice."

Merry wondered if he meant the wine or the birth of the baby. Barry could cram a whole conversation into one word.

He took a one hundred dollar bill from a gold clip. "Get a little something for the baby."

Ramon flashed a smile of appreciation that could light a stadium at midnight.

Merry considered what she knew about Barry. Generous, successful—and as scintillating as a cardboard cutout.

Merry, this is a business meeting. Not a personality assessment.

"The wine's wonderful," she said. "The label says it's from Australia. How did you find it?"

"I was there last year. I sent a few cases home. I keep some here too."

"You travel a lot?"

"Business." Silence was observed for at least twenty seconds. "Let's eat."

Apparently, lunch had been preordered. Two waiters swooped in with trays of lobsters, asparagus, fresh greens, and a choice of desserts. *Barry certainly does not like to waste time,* Merry thought. She wondered what it would be like to be so certain of everything. He was like a tank rolling through underbrush.

"I was thinking," he said as the waiter served their coffee, "you might take a look at another project I'm working on. We could drive out there after lunch."

"Another place like Randy's?"

"It's mine. An entirely different concept. A tract development—a planned community—in West Palm."

It apparently did not occur to him that she might have other afternoon plans. Barry, she mused, was animal, vegetable, and mineral. A man, a tree, and a tank. His cardboard facade was strictly for identification purposes.

"Yes, I'd like to see it."

"Good. Finished?"

She nodded.

The waiter pulled her chair out, and Barry started toward the door. No bill, no tip. Once outside, he mentioned that they billed him and included the tip. It saved time.

The car was waiting to take them to see the project. "Ever hear of Chadwick Farms?" Barry didn't wait for an answer. "It's an over fifty-five community of three hundred home sites, with twenty furnished models. We opened in September and sold two hundred. Phase three starts in May."

Merry just listened. There was nothing to say.

The serenity of Palm Beach soon disappeared as the Aston Martin became just another thread in the tapestry of rushing traffic. Gone were the palm trees, mansions, and serene apartment houses. Large billboards announced the coming of new housing tracts. Fruit and vegetable stands, trailer parks, and strip malls proclaimed the dreary existence of those living along this paved stretch of gloom.

Within a few minutes, the roadside scene changed to a series of homes, their rooftops barely visible above the high stuccoed walls that protected them from the rest of the world. Tasteful billboards lured prospective buyers to retirement Shangri-La's. "Casa Bonita, from $100,000. Premium lakeside lots available." "Villagio La Scala—authentic Italian villas. Swimming pool, clubhouse, tennis courts. From $250,000. Last phase." One after another, the developments lined up like entrants in a beauty contest. Merry had never seen anything like this before. Life in the middle of nowhere.

"What do people do out here?" she asked.

"Retire."

"Of course."

"Want to listen to some music? Carl, put on tape three."

The whining twang of a country ballad filled the silence.

> She broke my heart when she ran off with the plumber,
>
> And right now, I've never felt number.
>
> Now I'm alone, forever, I fear,
>
> So I sit at the bar and nurse a beer.
>
> Oh, I am a shambles, I am a mess.
>
> I shouldn't have hit her, I must confess.
>
> But there at the end of the bar
>
> Sits a pretty gal singing with a guitar,
>
> Wearing spangled jeans, looking like a star.
>
> My heart is jumpin' and spinnin' in me.
>
> Lordy lord, I think this gal's my destiny.

Merry wondered if there wasn't some benefit to being deaf.

"How'd you like it?" Barry asked.

"I'm not much of a music critic."

"My gardener's son Jimmie wrote it. He's sixteen. This kid's going places."

Hopefully, out of earshot.

"This is it. Chadwick Farms. Fountains, lakes, club-houses, tennis, and golf."

"Looks interesting."

"Used to be a vegetable farm. More profitable now as real estate. We can't build them fast enough to keep up with the demand. I'll show you the models."

Chadwick Farms featured small homes that resembled mansions if viewed from a distance. Merry was struck by the impeccable detail and quality. The basic models included granite counters in the kitchens, Jacuzzis, tile or parquet floors, marble baths, and intercoms. The upgrades featured marble floors, imported moldings, carved fireplace mantels, marble-fronted bars, and hidden safes. The homes were a bargain at $300,000 to $450,000. Most buyers, Barry said, added all the available upgrades.

Merry wondered where she would be living when she retired. Probably back in Boston at the Standish.

"Barry, the place is wonderful. The decorations and furnishings are magnificent. The houses are unbelievable."

"They are nice. Have you ever decorated in a development?"

"All my work up to now has been city apartments and suburban homes."

"That's interesting." He consulted his watch. "It's almost five o'clock. We'll head back now."

Back in the car, Barry pulled out a briefcase from a compartment on the back of the driver's seat and took a folder from the briefcase. "Take a look at these when you get back to the hotel. Tell me what you think. I'll call you tomorrow. We can discuss it over drinks. Around four should be good. You don't have any plans, have you?"

"I didn't until now. What do you want me to tell you?"

"If you like the sketches for the next phase. See if you can make any improvements."

"Barry, I don't think I should. Any time I spend on work is going to be on Randy's project."

"I know that. I know that. All I want is your personal opinion."

"Have you shown the sketches to other decorators for personal opinions?"

"Not yet. I want to hear your opinion first." He snapped the briefcase shut and put it back in the folding compartment. "Carl, put on some quiet music."

The rest of the way back was in comfortable silence.

Thirty-One

January 1995

Around seven that evening, Merry walked over to Breezy's for a sandwich and some iced tea. When she walked in, she was greeted as one of the regulars. Service was quick, and she was out within half an hour.

In her suite, she reviewed the events of the day. Barry and Randy were both treating her as if the house she was decorating were her own. No comments, no questions. She decided to take a quick look at Barry's folder. There were small sketches for the model houses to be started in May. They were far grander than the houses currently offered.

Merry let her imagination take her through each of the ten models. What would it be like to live in one of these places? Who would she be living with? She promised herself that when she returned to Manhattan at the end of April, she would finally decorate her Manhattan apartment if she meant to stay in the city.

She put Barry's folder down, intending to resume working on some ideas she had for Randy's palace. An envelope fell from the folder and onto the floor. She reached down to pick it up. Much to her surprise, it was addressed to her.

Merry,

You've probably noticed I'm a man of few words. Since we have a mutual working relationship with Randy, I don't want anything to interfere with that. But I enjoy your company. I'll pick you up at four on Sunday—tomorrow. I want to hear what you think about Chadwick Farms. I have theater tickets, if you'd like to go.

Barry

She read the note again, and then again. *What is this supposed to mean? Did he think I was coming on to him? I never gave that impression. I'm here to work on a job. And that's it. No entanglements. The conceit of that guy! Do I want to go to the theater? I don't want to go anywhere with him.*

She read the note one more time. Maybe she had misinterpreted what he meant. *Still,* Merry continued with her self-inflicted torment, *it just might be his way of being...*

Will you give it a rest? If only I had someone practical to talk to.

A nagging thought raced through her mind. *Am I always going to hurt myself before I might or might not actually get hurt? The guy didn't ask me to marry him. All he did was invite me to see a show. Read the letter, dummy. It says a "working relationship." You can read, can't you?*

Damn, damn, damn. I'm over forty, and I still don't know how to react.

She climbed under the sheets, socked her pillow once or twice, and endured a fitful sleep.

Although it was almost noon when Merry finally woke up, circles under her eyes announced her lack of sleep. A headache punctuated her discomfort. This was not going to be a day in paradise. Even though the sun streamed through the window, she felt miserable.

The quiet atmosphere in the suite was getting on her nerves. *Maybe I shouldn't have taken on this project. What was the matter with what I was doing before I jumped at Randy's consolation job? This isn't a consolation for anything... wake up.* Merry slid out of bed. *I'm going nuts,* she told herself.

When she greeted her reflection in the mirror, she saw a weary-looking woman with heavy eyes, a sleep-creased face, and a case of such bad bed-hair, it looked like a dead cat was perched on her head.

And good morning to you too. Merry laughed at herself. *Kiddo, you're really cracking up.*

Her coffee and the Sunday paper arrived minutes after she requested it. One sip of the aromatic brew, and she was ready to do some sketches for Randy's solarium. That was her favorite place in the little palace. She envisioned the oval room, with its expanse of windows and domed glass ceiling, furnished in casual bamboo-framed sofas in soft colors that reflected the changing colors of the sky and the ocean. A small fountain surrounded with tropical plantings would add to the illusion of the room, extending into the outdoors.

Her concentration was jarred by the ringing of the telephone.

"Hello?"

"Merry? Barry. You got my note?"

"Yes."

"What about the theater tonight?"

"Only if it's a comedy." Her response was not the one she'd intended.

"It's supposed to be very funny. So you'll go?"

"Sounds like fun."

"See you at four."

She returned to her sketching. A chandelier suspended from the glass dome would be a nice touch. She penciled it in.

When she arrived downstairs, she found Barry talking to a couple standing near the reception desk. From the intensity of the conversation, they seemed to be good friends. She walked over and greeted him.

Barry introduced her with a simple, "Merry Venture is decorating the Grant place."

"Ashok Bahadur." The tall, exotically handsome Indian man extended his hand. "And this is Fiona Ghiberti, our bookkeeper and major domo."

Fiona extended her own delicate hand, revealing long, tapered fingers ending in perfect oval-shaped nails. The ring finger of her left hand was ornamented with a marquise diamond solitaire the size of an area rug.

"Ashok manages the hotel," Barry said. "Fiona's husband Fabrizio does the legal work. The four of us own the place. You should have seen it when we bought it six years ago. I'll show you the pictures sometime."

He abruptly turned to Ashok and Fiona. "See you later. Miss Venture and I have a meeting."

Fiona smiled at Merry. Merry easily translated the expression as, "Oh, yes, a meeting."

The Silver Shadow was not in sight. In its place stood a white Excalibur convertible, with a burled walnut dashboard and a leather steering wheel. A Sunday kind of car.

Barry opened the door and handed Merry an orange box tied with brown ribbons. "Put the scarf on. The wind will blow your hair around."

She recognized the orange box and brown ribbons as Hermès's signature colors. Other signature combinations flashed through her mind: Tiffany used pale robin's-egg-blue boxes tied with white satin ribbon, and Cartier used red leather boxes with gold tooling. If the recipients of these gifts happened to be illiterate, the colors of the boxes were hints for the appropriate amount of appreciation.

Merry put the scarf on. "I'll return it at the end of the day." In no way was she going to consider this a gift.

"I always keep a scarf in this car," he said.

Definitely not a gift.

Barry pulled the car into the driveway of the Doric. His arrival was not unnoticed. Even at the Doric, an Excalibur created a sensation. The valets all but fell over themselves as they jumped to open the doors for Merry and Barry. Merry's Hermès scarf and dark glasses only added to the curiosity of the bystanders.

The Doric Hotel looked comfortable with itself. No glitz. Just carpets as luxurious as sable and sofas as comfortable as upholstered clouds. Marble-topped bombé chests tastefully festooned with gold-patina bronze garlands completed the intended effect. Understatements in elegance.

Barry steered Merry into a large clublike room filled with white-clothed tables and settees at which couples, families, and dowagers were having afternoon tea.

"Thought this might be nicer than sitting outside. I like coming here before the theater. It's just across the bridge."

"What time is the show?"

"At eight."

It was not quite five o'clock. *Three hours of sitting with Mr. Conversation—how lucky can I get?* Merry was not surprised when a waiter deposited a tray of tea sandwiches, a teapot, and a small stand laden with teacakes. Another waiter placed an ice bucket on the table and immediately offered a glass of champagne for Barry's approval.

"Shall I be mother?" Merry asked as she started to pour the tea.

Raising his glass, Barry said, "Don't you want some champagne first?"

"I'm really not much of a drinker."

The waiter appeared again and filled Merry's glass, but tea really was all Merry wanted. "The tea's good."

"You ought to taste this stuff. It's very good."

"Just a sip."

It was good. Perhaps it was the sleepless night that was putting her on edge. A nagging sensation kept picking at her as she drank more tea.

"Is something bothering you?" Barry asked. "You look distressed."

"I do? I'm not. Why?"

"You seem preoccupied. Like you're somewhere else. If you don't like it here, we can leave. Just say so."

"No. Really, everything's fine. I worked late last night, so I'm a bit tired."

"You should eat something. You'll feel better. Would you rather have something else? I'll get the waiter."

"Please, don't. Would you excuse me for minute?"

"Don't run away." He picked up a small tea sandwich.

Merry walked out of the room and headed for the ladies' lounge, where she slumped on one of the tufted leather sofas and burst into tears.

A stunningly dressed woman at the next table noticed her. "Can I get you a glass of water?"

"No, thank you. I'll feel better in a minute or two. I'm just overtired."

The woman sat down next to Merry. "More tears are shed in the Doric ladies' lounge. We should all get together and have an annual reunion."

Merry took her head out of her hands and looked in the mirror. "Oh, my God, just look at me. I'm a mess."

"You're with Barry Chadwick. I saw the two of you having tea. By the way, I'm Nell Porter."

Merry introduced herself and started to repair her red eyes.

"Barry and my husband Holt are great friends. They usually fly to Nassau together on weekends. If you're going back now, I'll join you and say hello to Barry."

When the two women returned, they found Barry and another man deep in conversation.

"I see you found each other," Barry said. He sounded pleased. He turned to the man with him. "Holt, meet Merry Venture. She's doing the Grant property."

What an incredibly handsome couple, Merry thought. Both Nell and Holt were lightly tanned, with complexions that were the magical results of frequent facials. Holt, over six feet tall, with chiseled features and fashion-magazine-worthy salt-and-pepper hair, contrasted with petite Nell with her burnished auburn hair. Her delicate cameo face was dominated by a pair of enormous emerald-green eyes framed by long, thick black lashes. Both Nell and Holt smiled warmly at Merry. Nell took Merry's hand and said, "We won't keep you from your tea. Holt and I have to get home to our guests."

Holt shook Barry's hand. Nell gave Merry an air kiss on the cheek and vanished, leaving a trail of Patou's Sublime fragrance.

"Let's finish our tea," Barry said. He said little more, only the occasional comment that she should try this or that little sandwich. Since Merry had nothing to say, this quiet interlude suited her mood. But she could not fathom why he was paying so much attention to her. Theirs was strictly a working relationship, and she certainly did not want it to go any further.

After half an hour or so, which seemed to Merry like an eternity, Barry asked her if she would like to take a walk. Before she could finish saying, "I could use the exercise," he had beckoned for the check. While he strode toward the door, he took Merry's arm.

"We've been invited to their party. We'll take a tin of pâté over to Nell and Holt's. Bice will fix it up for me." Barry, it seemed, assumed she was going with him.

Who's the we? Where? When? Careful, Merry warned herself. "I think I'd better let you know," she said. "I'll be at the dealers tomorrow, so I'll be working on my orders tomorrow night."

"But that's Monday. I'm talking about Wednesday. Don't you want to go?"

She detected a note of disappointment in his voice.

"I'd love to." Again, what came out of her mouth was a complete surprise. This relationship was exclusively professional, and that is the way Merry wanted it to remain.

"Good. Nell and Holt make a great couple. She's a big supporter of the arts. Holt is a benefactor to hospitals and local charities. He's my tennis partner."

"Nell told me you and Holt usually fly down to Nassau on the weekends."

"All that information in five minutes in the ladies' lounge?"

"She saw us having tea and introduced herself to me."

"That's Nell. What else did you gals talk about?"

"Nothing, actually. We were just freshening up."

"But what does 'Nothing, actually' mean?" Barry asked with a quizzical smile.

"Just that. 'Hello, I'm Nell.' 'I'm Merry.'"

"That's the one thing about women we all want to know—what kind of talk goes on in the ladies' lounge."

"Nothing, really." Merry smiled.

"That's the first time you've smiled. For a while there, I thought you might not have any teeth."

She looked at Barry and smiled again. *Don't tell me the tree is sprouting a personality.*

"Let's take a walk," he said. "We have some time before the show."

They crossed the street to the Seagrape Center, where shop windows displayed exquisite luxury items, from yacht and golf attire to fine jewelry. The area was not crowded, and the weekend shoppers were gone. A few couples sat at tables outside an ice cream shop. Others strolled, looking in the shop windows. Old couples, young couples. Couples. Merry wondered if she and Barry looked like a couple. But they were invisible to the others, who were engrossed with ice cream, looking in the shop windows and their own lives.

Barry was a good host. Generous and thoughtful. But remote. Merry gave herself a mental kick. *Barry is treating you this way because both of you are under contract to Randy.*

"You look deep in thought," he said.

"No, I was just enjoying the surroundings. It's so different from all the noise and dust of Manhattan."

"Do you miss it?"

"Not really. I'll be here until April, but if I finish the house earlier, I'll go back sometime in March."

"Too bad. You'll miss the spring weather. Want a cone before we drive over to the theater?"

"Sounds good to me."

Somehow the length of time with Barry that Merry had dreaded eased into a comfortable time of eating ice cream, just like the other people enjoying a lovely Sunday.

A quick ride across the bridge, and they were in front of an old schoolhouse that had been converted into a community theater. The play was an original comedy written by a local playwright. It was hilarious, but the noise level in the audience made the dialogue difficult to hear. A fierce competition of sound ran among the actors, the talkative audience, the echo created from the sound system, and the rattling of the antiquated air-conditioning system. Two women sitting behind them were more interested in their own conversation than in what the actors had to say.

"Have you heard from Sylvia?" one asked the other.

"She's not talking to me since the last game of mahjong."

"You're still playing?"

"Not a lot. Just every other morning, three afternoons, and four nights."

"So what's going to happen? You're still playing with her?"

"I have no choice. She drives."

They also overheard snippets of other conversations:

"Sh-h-h. We can't hear the show."

"It's so hot in here. It's like a steam bath."

"Wanna go for coffee after?"

"Not at that hour. I get gas."

Barry whispered to Merry, "Had enough?"

"Absolutely."

They climbed their way to the aisle, attempting not to trip over feet. "Sorry. Excuse us."

"We're trying to watch the play! Some people are so inconsiderate."

Once outside, Merry and Barry broke into laughter.

They drove back across the bridge and headed up South Ocean Boulevard toward the Palm Crest Inn. Merry couldn't believe the awesome spectacle created by the silver moon floating in the black velvet sky. Stars sparkled like crystals in a celestial chandelier. Little blue and green lights hidden in the shrubbery illuminated the mansions' exteriors, while an amber radiance glowed in the windows of these palaces. It wasn't real—none of it. It was an impossible dream.

Barry was quiet, and Merry was so absorbed in the tropical atmosphere that she was surprised when they arrived at her hotel.

Barry turned off the motor and said, "Listen, I want to tell you something. I'm not going to be seeing you after Wednesday. I'm going to Texas for a couple of days on business. Do you mind?"

"I don't mind."

You need to set him straight, Merry told herself. *Right now. Just say, "I'm here on an assignment with a deadline, so I really don't have time for anything but work. But this was fun, and I appreciate your showing me around."*

All she said was, "Well, it's late, and I have a busy week ahead of me. So I'll say good night."

"Don't forget Wednesday night at Nell and Holt's." Barry got out of the car and walked Merry to the door. "I had a good time."

"So did I," she said.

"Good night again." Barry smiled. Then he and the Excalibur disappeared into the night.

Thirty-Two

January 1995

By ten o'clock Monday morning, Merry was on her way across the bridge to her first appointment on Antique Row in West Palm Beach. The traffic was a tangle of trucks, cars, and motorcycles, braiding their way along the highway with little regard for the posted speed limits. Merry was determined to concentrate on her driving as she struggled to dismiss her thoughts about the time spent with Barry.

One of these days, she decided, she was going to treat herself to a hit on the head with a baseball bat. Why had she gone out with him in the first place? She wasn't that lonely. She'd call and cancel for Wednesday. She had to focus on work and get this project done before April.

"Hey, lady, will you look where you're driving?" A shirtless, soda-drinking guy gave Merry the finger and sped off. Merry again applied herself to concentrating on getting to her destination.

The rest of the day went smoothly, and she was delighted with the treasures she found in the antique, consignment, and off-beat shops lining Antique Row. She was back to her hotel before five.

Once again, she had dinner at Breezy's. Monday was all-you-can-eat meat loaf night. On her walk back to the hotel, she was caught up in the delicious perfume of exotic flowers that bordered the storefront windows. Magnificent displays of oriental carpets, fine linens, imported clothing, antiques, leashes and beds for dogs, and fanciful children's clothing beckoned the evening stroller for a closer look. Even the police station was landscaped and lit as if it were a private club. *What do you have to do to get arrested around here? Drive a dirty car?* Merry was in a good mood—for an old maid. She always found it necessary to remind herself of her plight in life.

As she approached the glass door of the hotel, she could see the night clerk sitting at the reception desk, again engrossed in his Harley-Davidson catalog. She entered the lobby and headed toward the elevator.

"Don't you say hello?"

She whirled around at the sound of the familiar voice. "Randy, what are you doing here? I thought you were in London." She did not add that Caprice had told her that she had run into Randy in Tiffany.

"No hello hug?"

"Hello. Consider yourself hugged."

"Aren't you going to ask me up and give me a progress report?"

"Of course. I'm going to work for couple of hours anyway. Did you get the sketches I sent to the office?"

What Merry really wanted to say was, *Randy, I've missed you.* No, that wasn't the whole truth. But how could she blurt out, "Why can't we start over again?"

Because he's engaged, you idiot. You never had a chance with him, because each time there was a possibility, you did something to ruin it. Face it; any chance for romance between the both of you was only in your imagination.

Merry stopped berating herself as they got in the elevator. "I can send down for some wine, if you like," she offered.

"I'd like that."

"Good."

That was the extent of their conversation: "Want wine" and "Good." Were they quoting the English subtitles of a Japanese movie? What was next? "You sit. I pour?" She chuckled.

"What's so funny?" Randy asked.

"You really don't want to know."

"Something must be funny."

"You know—events of the day and all."

As they walked out of the elevator, Randy's voice took on a serious tone. "You seem deep in thought—remote. If I didn't know you better, I'd say you aren't telling me the truth. What's bothering you? I thought things were fine–the way you wanted them to be."

"Sometimes, we don't know the way things should be. We don't always know what we want."

"You're not sorry you took on this job, are you?"

Merry attempted a casual tone as she opened the door to her suite. "Here it is. My home away from home."

"Looks comfortable. Are you comfortable?"

"Yes. Very. I'll call for the wine. Any preference, Randy?"

"You pick."

She called and ordered Chardonnay. Then she put the most recent sketches on the coffee table and placed other sketches and the fabric samples in the center of the sofa.

"Oh, your side and my side?" he said, indicating the space she'd created between them on the sofa. Randy gave her a come-on-don't-be-like-that smile. "That looks nice and friendly."

"I think it will be easier to look at the sketches and the fabric samples that way, don't you?"

"No, I don't." He took the fabric samples and sketches off the sofa and put them under the coffee table. "Merry, don't you think it's time for us to have a truth hour?"

"Truth hour? About what?"

"About us. We're still friends, I hope."

"Yes. Of course. Why shouldn't we be friends?"

"Merry, has anyone ever told you that you're a damned fool?"

"I get the distinct feeling you are."

An avalanche of confusion heaped itself on her, leaving her breathless and bewildered over what Randy was going to do or say. Whatever it was, she didn't think she wanted to hear it. She had always been afraid of hearing something that might hurt her—something that would plunge her into that terrible feeling of despair, the feeling that she was going to be abandoned, ridiculed.

I'm my own worst enemy. I don't need anyone to hurt me when I can do it to myself before anyone gets to me. Look what I'm doing to myself—destroying my chances for happiness because I enjoy tormenting myself over things that are in the past; unimportant, meaningless things in the scheme of the life that I now live. When will I give myself a break?

"Merry, are you in there?" Randy waved his hand in front of her eyes.

"Sorry, I was caught up in a bit of nothingness. I'm here."

"Merry, you are a wonderful person—funny, bright, and not hard to look at. But you—and I hope you don't take this as a criticism but as a longtime observation from a real friend—you don't let anything penetrate you, to allow you to feel passion. You've shut yourself off—not just from me but from yourself. You have always been dear to me, but I have to move on. Over the years, I've tried to reach you, but you never really responded. So I gave up. Merry, I'm sorry. I really am. You know I loved you, and you… Well, I've said what I have to say."

Merry remained silent for some time, soaking in what Randy had just said. How would she—should she—respond to his honesty? All this from him coming out of thin air. What could she possibly say? "I'm afraid of being happy?" "I don't deserve love?" "I'm not worth anything to myself, let alone to a relationship?"

Tears streamed down her face. She felt old, lonely, and confronted, like a trapped animal. Randy had finally cornered her. Revealed her to herself—the self she thought she had so carefully hidden. She had fooled no one. She was the fooled.

"I didn't mean to hurt you," he said. "I really didn't. I needed to tell you the truth before we both went our separate ways. I had no intention of being cruel—of hurting you."

She looked at him with a new appreciation of how he truly was. But she had misread him through the warped lens with which she viewed her world of personal relationships. Now, when it was too late, she realized what she had thrown in her trash heap of missed opportunities.

"I don't know what to say," she said, "except that I'm sorry too—sorrier than you will ever know. If I confessed the depths of my feelings now, you probably wouldn't believe me, because of all my glibness in the past. What can I say? I didn't care? But the fact is, I think I was in love with you. It's just that I didn't want to get hurt, even though you never gave me any reason to think you would hurt me. I had to make sure I kept everything light so I wouldn't be disappointed. It's crazy, but that's the truth, and I'll have to live with it."

Even though her words conveyed one thing, her thoughts conveyed a message of ambivalence. Not of mistrust but of not being convinced that what she was saying now had any truth in it. Suddenly, she felt as if she were awake for the first time in her adult life, and she was in control of the punishing feelings of worthlessness she'd inflicted on herself. The haunting internal dialogues between her and mother, Glenda, had finally dissipated—gone at last. Ms. Merry Dawn Venture had emerged from the cocoon.

"I have to take some of the blame," Randy said, his soft voice sincere. "I should have told you how I felt at the start. But would it have made any difference?"

"Probably not. I've been locked up inside myself for so long that I don't have any real feelings. And that makes me sad—it really does."

It was not a lament over Randy. She was sad for her delayed maturity. Again, she wondered why she did not just say good-bye and move on. It was a strange curiosity, like driving past a car accident and realizing that if you slowed down to gape, another accident might happen.

"I never knew how you felt." He took her in his arms, and she began to cry as if her world had shattered. "Can you forgive me for being so blunt? Maybe I should have kept all this to myself."

She controlled her sobs and swiped tears from her face. "No, I'm glad we had a moment of truth with each other. I feel freer than I've felt in... well, ever. And I thank you for that. For the first time, I'm looking at myself, my life, as it really is. You don't know what a big favor—no, what a gift—you've given me."

He leaned back to look at her face. "Then you're okay? Really? You're not just saying that?"

"Randy, believe me when I tell you that this is the truth. No jokes or glib remarks. Just the plain, teary truth."

"We should have said this years ago."

"Perhaps, but we're going in different directions now. I have my work, and you'll be married soon. Life goes on, as trite as it seems. But I guess life *is* a series of cross-purpose intentions, unfulfilled dreams, and misread opportunities."

"It's too bad we weren't ever lovers. We should have taken the chance. But knowing what you just told me, it wouldn't have been likely."

She shook her head. "Then, no. Now it's too late. But I don't have any regrets. You and I have had an up-and-down relationship. We both survived it, and no real damage was done. I feel at peace with myself, now that we... now that I've been honest with you and myself."

"I don't think it's good-bye just yet. We do have a contract and a house to decorate. By the way, are you satisfied with how it's working out?"

"Shouldn't I be asking you that question? After all, it is your house."

"True, but I always like to give the artiste the license to create. And I did tell you to make it look like something you could live in."

"But I won't be living in it. Elizabeth will." For the first time, Merry truly acknowledged the existence of Randy's elusive fiancée.

He quickly changed the subject. "Do you think you'll need all four months to finish the house?"

The tone had changed. Business now. "Actually, no. The bathrooms and kitchen are to be installed by the end of the month, and I've ordered the furnishings. The contractor has scheduled the final cleanup in six weeks. All I have to do is hang around until everything is completed. Then I'll arrange the furniture, get the window treatments installed, and I'm done."

"Then why don't you come back to New York now? You can come back here later when you're needed again."

"I've thought of that, but my apartment is being used by Charles and Edward. They're managing the studio while I'm gone."

"Remember, there's a bonus if you finish early." Randy got up and walked around the living room. "You know, you never showed me the bedroom."

"It's that door. Have a look. It's a very comfortable room. The bath is next to it."

Randy opened the door and walked in. "It is a very cozy room. The bed is nice and soft." She heard him walk into the bathroom. "Why are you sitting out there? Aren't you going to show me how the swan works?"

"There's a handle. You can't miss it."

It was silent for a moment, and then Randy walked out of the bedroom and sat next to her on the small sofa. She moved away, but her heart was beating hard, and she felt on fire. "Randy, it's getting late, and I do have to work tomorrow."

"Tomorrow. This is now. Merry..." He took her into his arms and kissed her.

A thunderclap of emotions vibrated through Merry. She had no thoughts and became pliable in his arms as she responded to his kiss with warmth, passion, and desire.

Randy got up and, taking Merry by both hands, led her into the bedroom and sat her on the bed. She did not resist. He sat next to her and kissed her once again. Kissing her all the while, he lowered her gently. How he did it, Merry did not know, but the bedspread was out from under her, and she was slowly being undressed. Her breath came in small gasps as she melted to his touch.

He slid her under the covers, slipped off his clothes, and took her in his arms. "Merry, I love you, and I always have. This time, let me show you how I feel."

Her voice seemed to come from her body, which was far away, and it was as if the only part left was her desire. "Yes, love me, Randy. Love me."

It happened in stages of soft touches of exploration and hungry kisses—nothing rushed. Then suddenly, Merry cried out in ecstasy, while bursts of flames and shudders coursed through her in wave after wave of release from everything she had ever known. It was a rebirth, a new awakening. It was joy.

Randy held her while both of them breathed in and out in unison. They stayed wrapped in each other's arms, enjoying the closeness, the silent intimacy, and a contentment that erased all of her past. They were on the threshold of now.

Randy spoke first. "Merry, this is your first time, isn't it?"

"Yes," she replied in a small voice.

"You're all right? I didn't hurt you, did I?"

"It was wonderful. And I do love you for being so kind, so understanding, so... wonderful."

What did all this mean? Should she think...? *Don't think, Merry. Stay in the present. Enjoy your glimpse of paradise.* She stretched out on the bed, reveling in the moment.

"Merry, do you realize it's five in the morning?"

"I don't realize anything. I'm no longer on this planet."

He kissed her. "We'd better clean up. You go first."

When she emerged from the bathroom, she felt she must be glowing. The ground beneath her feet did not exist. She couldn't stop smiling with the triumph of discovery. *At last,* she told herself, *I feel real, part of life.* She smoothed the bedcovers and sat on top of them, wishing that tomorrow would never come—but it did. Just as Randy walked out of the bathroom, dawn was coloring the vanishing nighttime sky.

Randy dressed in the living room while Merry—with great reluctance—put on her clothes. Randy didn't bother to ask her if she was dressed. He just walked into the bedroom and kissed her. "That's for good morning."

She kissed him back. He tasted like toothpaste and smelled of scented soap. Delicious.

Coffee and rolls were always available at any hour from room service, so she ordered some. She was surprised when the clerk asked if she wanted eggs, toast, and fruit too. Breakfast for two was delivered with Damson plum jam and tiny Danish pastries. They ate slowly, with great satisfaction.

Finally, Randy said he had to go. He had an early flight back to New York.

"I can drive you. I have a car."

"So do I, and there are some things I have to do before I go. I'll call you before I leave. One more thing. Think about coming back early. You've got most of the work done, and you can come back down here to finish up when the time comes."

"I will. But this weather can be quite seductive."

"It won't be a problem, traveling back and forth."

"That's not the problem. As I told you, the problem is that two people from La Viola are living in my apartment while I'm gone."

"Try to work it out." He winked at her and was gone.

Merry hung the Do Not Disturb sign on her door and sat on her bed, pulling her knees up close. How could this have happened? And what now?

Just let it go, she advised herself. *It was your one-time invitation to join the living. Get him out of your thoughts and get on with your life. You're a grown-up. This is what grown-ups do. Even if it's only once.*

Not more than a half hour elapsed before the telephone rang, barging in on Merry's musing. "Hello?"

"Merry? Randy." Before she could reply, he continued, "Can you arrange to be in the city on Friday? There are some things we'll need to go over."

"I could. Is something the matter?"

"Why should there be anything the matter? Take an early flight and be here by noon. I'll pick you up at the airport."

"I don't have any place to stay."

"Will you stop worrying about things for once? I'll take care of it. Just be back Friday at noon. My flight's being called. I'll see you on Friday."

What was that all about? she wondered. Was she about to get fired? *Merry, dear, just because you slept with your boss doesn't mean he can't fire you.* Maybe he'd run out of money and had to make do with a partially furnished mansion. Whatever it was, returning to New York would be a break from the incessantly beautiful weather and peace and quiet. She really could use a fix of loud, honking taxis and a whiff or two of traffic exhaust.

She stretched out on the bed and fell asleep. It was a sleep that conjured up a recurrent dream that catapulted her back to a time when she felt most alone and helpless. Years had passed since those days, yet they plagued her in her sleep. Not once did she stop to examine what message these dream phantoms might be able to reveal.

Thirty-Three

January 1995

Glenda Venture hurled her baby Merry into the Venture universe, where lessons in failure, insecurity, fear, and isolation were punctuated by a constant litany of dissatisfaction, envy, anger, and suspicion. These were preached from the pulpit of the black stove, which dominated the kitchen of the sanctuary called home.

"Don't put on yoah Sunday mannuhs for me, Miss Phony. I'm on to ya. And so is yoah fahthah. I don't know who ya think ya ahr, but ya certainly don't get it from heah."

"All I asked you was if you'd like to chaperone the dance at school."

"Listen, missy, I'm not chaperoning anything with those phonies. Some of those parents think they ahr fancy because they went to college and drive their own cahrs. But would they say hello to you on the street? Nevah. So fancy. 'Glenda, when ya put ahr order in, please tell them to leave the crusts off the sandwich.' Do they want me to chew it for them too?"

"Mama, they didn't mean anything by it. Lots of people don't like crust on their sandwiches."

"And since when did you become a membah of the country club?"

"I was only trying to tell you something. That was all. Really, that was all."

"Well, ya don't have to tell me anything. I know all I have to know. I'm on to them, and they know it. And yoah not going to any dance so that boys can take advantage of ya. Now go set the table."

"Yes, mama."

"What's the mattah now?"

"Nothing."

"No sense in sulking. Too many girls get pregnant at sixteen."

"From a school dance?"

"Do you want peas?"

"Anything. I don't care."

"We're not having any tramps in this house; that I can tell ya right now."

"I'm not a tramp."

"Then don't talk like one. Dances, beah, God knows what all."

"What makes you an authority?"

"Watch yoah mouth, or I'll tell your fahthah when he gets home."

"I wish you would."

"That's enough from you, thank ya very much."

"Mama, don't you love me?"

"Every muthah loves her child. The ideas you come up with!"

"Couldn't I go to the dance?"

"Any more of yoah cheap talk and you'll go to bed without suppah."

"Who wants to eat that shit anyway."

"For that big mouth, yoah being punished."

"I thought I already was."

Merry woke with a start and sat bolt upright. The dream had followed her to her hotel in Palm Beach. The recurrent dream about a life she had lived long ago—so long ago that the memory of it should have faded. But she kept stoking the embers, which caused those sooty days to live on.

Merry, you are a complete idiot. You are no more that pathetic, frightened girl than you are a failure in your life. Look at what you have accomplished. Look at yourself, not as you see yourself, but how you really are. You've blinded yourself by looking at the charred remains of the past. It's gone. Leave it and move on. And while you're at it, how about not anticipating the worst before anything ever happens? Give yourself a rest. You might like it.

It was time, Merry realized, for her real self to emerge. *Okay,* she thought, *one, two, three... ta-da! Ladies and gentlemen, I introduce to you the new Merry Dawn Venture.*

With that, Merry bounded out of bed to start the day.

Thirty-Four

January 1995

By Wednesday afternoon, Merry had completed most of the orders for the house. Sketches, fabric selections, and measurements for the window treatments were sent off to La Viola. They promised the work would be completed in eight weeks. A crew from La Viola would fly down from Boston to install everything. For the moment, she had the luxury of contemplating what to do for the rest of the day, before Barry picked her up to go to Nell and Holt's. Shopping. Why not go shopping for something to wear that night?

Worth Avenue, the Gold Cup of shopping experiences, never disappointed the big-league shopper. It was the street of heart's desires, the rich dessert without the calories, the ultimate shopping orgasm. It was the place where being a bag lady meant carrying logo-laden sacks from designer shops and exotic boutiques—especially from Chanel, Valentino, Cartier, or Tiffany. A bag from each, of course, was even better.

The sun beat down on the street, bathing the elegant storefronts with a transcendental light. Women wore large straw hats to shade their newly rejuvenated, acid-peeled pale faces. The only thing wrinkled on Worth Avenue that day was a Shar-Pei puppy ambling down the street on the end of a Louis Vuitton leash.

Merry wandered into a small boutique in the Esplanade, where she treated herself to a simple little nothing of a dress and a pair of slides with lethal-weapon high heels. Once outside, she realized that if she gained one ounce, the dress wouldn't fit. But after splurging on it, she wouldn't be able to afford to eat for a month.

That evening, as Barry escorted Merry to his Silver Shadow, he looked at her with new interest, as if he were seeing her for the first time.

"You know, you look stunning tonight. Really beautiful. And you seem different, more relaxed."

"I do? How? I feel the same." *What a liar you are, Merry. What a liar.*

"What are you smiling about? Merry, you are absolutely glowing. Or is it my imagination?"

"No. It's just that I feel happy. My work is getting done, and the weather and the company are good. Why shouldn't I glow?"

"Well, keep it up. It becomes you."

All the way down South Ocean Boulevard, the Silver Shadow commanded the road, creating its own regal procession. Luis, in his chauffeur's uniform and cap, handled the vehicle with an air of superiority known only among the ranks of staff drivers. Luis worked exclusively for Barry Chadwick, and that steady employment provided him status by association.

When the car reached its destination, Merry was astonished by a sight that eclipsed the other oceanfront "cottages" they had passed on the way. The massive French-chateau–style structure was not obscured from the road by masses of tall hedges, as were some of the other homes. This pink granite palace rested comfortably atop a wide, graceful marble staircase that led to a pair of enormous glass and bronze doors that provided a view straight through the house to the ocean. All the landscaping captured the beauty of the natural environment, just as the bronze sculptures, fountains, and walkways were placed to enhance, not dominate, the grounds. In addition, a pair of huge windows flanking the front and back of an upper-floor gallery allowed passersby a glimpse of the ever-present sky. It might have been viewed as beyond belief, but this was a reality—at least, for Nell and Holt.

Nell and Holt Porter were a great team. After fifteen years of marriage, Nell referred to Holt as her first husband. Holt called her his bride. They never stopped being in love—and everyone loved them. Their mutual generations of inherited wealth had long removed the frustrations and insecurities that plagued anxious social neophytes. Nell was placid; Holt was relaxed. Together they were considerate, generous, and thoughtful. It was a given that the Porters would buy two tables at charity balls. The ballet, the opera, and local museums said the Porters were "like family."

When Nell first encountered the tearful Merry in the Doric ladies' lounge, it didn't take her long to realize that here was an ordinary woman in an overwhelming situation. Nell recognized the tears, if not the participant. It wasn't the first time she had seen social insecurities reduce hopeful women to tears as they glimpsed at a world that for some was a reality, but for them was beyond a barrier they would never surmount.

It had been a coincidence that Nell and Merry were in the lounge at the same time, but Nell had a talent for gathering a disparate collection of acquaintances into her universe. Many an insecure woman had been rescued by Nell at luncheons and other social functions. Most were only too happy to be asked to address envelopes and make telephone calls for Nell's charity events.

A few were fortunate enough to actually marry into her rarefied world. Not all of them remembered to repay Nell's kindness to others. Nell laughed it off. "Beware of the servant who becomes the queen." Gratitude was the other person's concern.

Nell and Holt's guests gathered on the broad marble and granite terrace that overlooked an eternity pool, which seemed to be part of the ocean. The house and the acres of unending palm trees, terraces, fountains, and gardens dwarfed the hundred guests.

As soon as Nell and Holt saw Merry and Barry, they came over to greet them. "I'm so glad to see both of you," Nell said. "And Merry, you look positively glowing."

"I told her the same thing," Barry said, "and she tells me it's because she finishing up her work." This was a very long sentence for Barry.

"Really?" Nell gave Merry a "so-what's-the-secret?" look.

Merry just smiled. "The company and the climate have a good effect on me."

"I'd sure like to see you when you're ecstatic."

"I promise you, Nell, you'll be the first one to know."

Barry put his arm around Merry in a protective way and gave her a little squeeze. Merry responded by looking up at him and smiling.

"Barry," Holt said, "let's leave the girls to their glow talk. How about a drink?"

"You read my mind, Holt, buddy. Merry, you still having Chardonnay?"

"Sure, why not?"

Barry and Holt strolled off to the bar, stopping on the way to say a few words to everyone they encountered. Almost all the guests were old friends.

"Merry, come with me. I want you to meet some of my partners in crime." Nell took Merry by the arm and walked her over to a group of slim women who were deep in conversation. "Girls, meet Merry Venture. She's new here, so be nice."

Everyone laughed in a friendly way. When Nell said, "Be nice," she wasn't joking. Nell would not tolerate her friends treating one another in a shabby way. Of course, no one ever did. Who would dare risk banishment from this Olympic height of social success?

It was important to Nell that close friends be exactly that. Her reasoning was simple, and everyone she knew respected it. She reasoned that to have so much and yet squabble over who was to sit where and who was to do what first was a waste of time. It was, in her own words, an abuse of being privileged. That was how she'd been brought up, and that was that.

Introductions flew around Merry's head. Of the ten women in the little cluster, she recognized eight of them from their pictures in the "Social Spotlite." Up close, these women were astonishingly beautiful, like exotic flowers that would wither if ever placed in the harsh reality of a strip mall discount store.

The usual "Where are you from?" and "Have you met...?" and "Have you been to...?" questions were all asked in a warm, friendly manner. Merry apparently answered to the satisfaction of all, and she was then drawn into the previous conversation.

"I was just telling everyone," one woman said, "that I can't play golf tomorrow because I'm going to Argentina. Do you play, Merry? You could fill in for me."

Before Merry could respond, a woman named Tandy asked, "Why tomorrow, Carrie? We planned this game a month ago."

"Take it up with Griffin. He's the one who wants me to run his errand tomorrow. I asked him if I could go some other time, but the horse auction is on Friday, and he wants me to be there and make sure ours is the final bid."

"Why doesn't he go himself?" Merry felt secure enough in her standing with Nell to join in.

"They're putting the finishing touches on his new boat, and he wants to supervise the Jacuzzi installation. I'll go, I told him, but please don't complain that I'm the extravagant one. All I did was put in a larger kitchen and a new solarium. You'd think I was paving A1A from Jupiter to Miami."

Everyone laughed. Carrie filled Merry in, saying that her kitchen had been getting tired looking. It hadn't been done in five years. And the new solarium really had been a necessity. Anyone who thought they could pack twelve round tables in the old solarium wasn't being realistic. She finished by asking Merry if she could fill in for her.

"I'm sorry to say I don't play golf. I'm not much of a sportswoman."

"Nonsense," Carrie said. "If you don't want to play tomorrow, you'll be my guest at the club when I get back. If you like it, maybe you'll take lessons."

"Why wait until you get back?" another woman, named Tinka, asked. "Merry can have lunch with us when we finish the game."

"I'd like to, but I'm on a tight schedule," Merry said. "I'm down here as the decorator of the Grant place."

"I've heard about it," Tinka said. "It's supposed to be darling. Only twelve rooms, but the views from the windows are supposed to be spectacular."

The conversation shifted as one woman asked another, "Didn't you buy a house recently?"

"We close next month."

"Did you buy in Jupiter?"

"No, Paris."

A chime announced that dinner was now being served in the solarium, which held twenty tables and had a semicircular stage for the band.

It was a magical, starlit evening, complete with soft breezes and a platinum moon. The salty ocean spray mingled with the fragrance of tropical flowers, while palm trees swayed in unison, as if to an unseen conductor. Happy voices tinkled across the terrace and mingled with the ping of crystal goblets raised in toasts to friendship and love.

Merry and Barry stood at the edge of the eternity pool and gazed into the darkness over the ocean. In the distance, the lights on a cruise ship glistened. The rhythmic lapping of the ocean against the shore was soothing to the point of being hypnotic. Barry put his arm around Merry, and she rested her head against his shoulder. They said nothing for quite some time, as if their voices would spoil the mood.

Slowly, Barry turned Merry toward him and, raising her head, he kissed her.

"Merry, I've been wanting to do that all night. There is something so different about you, so relaxed and warm. It's as if you've undergone some kind of transformation. You weren't like this when we first met." He held her closer to him and kissed her again.

"I think I have changed," she said. "Or maybe awakened. It's a long story and not a very interesting one. Let's just say I feel comfortable when I'm with you."

"Do you want to take a walk on the beach?"

"That would be lovely."

"Can you walk in those things you're wearing?"

"I can take them off. See?"

The beach area that bordered the six-acre property was groomed with sand as white and soft as flour. Barry slipped off his loafers and placed them on a step leading down to the ocean. Merry did the same with her shoes.

They walked hand in hand as the breeze danced around them like a playful elf, sprinkling ocean spray in their faces. Barry stopped walking and took Merry in his arms again. They stood as still as the bronze sculptures that decorated the terrace at the top of the stairs.

"Merry, I don't even know if there's anyone in your life. Is there?"

"No, there isn't." She knew she wasn't just saying that. It was the truth. What had happened with Randy was an event that finally closed the door on their long, uneasy, and—Merry now realized—immature relationship. Making love with Randy had released her from her old self. She felt as if she had stepped across a threshold and entered a new territory of endless possibilities.

"You know," Barry said, "neither of us are kids. Maybe we could have a future together or at least give it a try. What do you think, Merry?"

"Right now, I'm not thinking anything. And I've never thought about a future with someone. But if you like, I will think about it."

"I like, and I want you to." He took her by the hand, and they continued their walk in silence.

Then, in a quiet voice, Barry said, "You know a lot of women have tried for years to get me. I'm not saying that to be boastful. It's true. A single guy who happens to be, well, to be modest... No, I'm not going to play around. Merry. I'm a very wealthy man."

"My God, the way you say that, you'd think you have something catching."

All of a sudden, both of them were laughing. "What does a guy have to do to impress you?"

"You'll be the first to know."

"Let's say good night to our host and hostess, and then we'll go for a drive. Better yet, let's take a French leave. They'll never miss us."

"Yes, let's." There was a sudden breathless quality to her voice.

As they got into the Rolls, Barry instructed Luis to drive to the house. They would leave Luis there, and Barry would take Merry home.

In the car, Barry put his arm around Merry. She looked out the window and thought the stars were dancing in the sky.

Barry's Regency-style white-stucco house was on the beach side of the road, which was unusual. Most of the houses were across the street, with beach access through underground tunnels. The one-story house featured windows with ocean views from all the rooms, while a sweeping terrace of pink marble and a pool house completed the estate.

"This is it," he said as Luis pulled under the porte cochère. Barry helped Merry out of the car, and Luis took the vehicle to the five-car garage.

"Let's go in. I'll make some coffee." Holding Merry's hand, he led her to the front door. A housekeeper opened the door as soon as they approached it.

"Mrs. Adams, this is Miss Venture. You can go now. I'll lock up." He turned to Merry. "The kitchen's this way." Still holding her hand, he walked her through the house. "Well, what do you think?" he asked when they reached the kitchen.

Barry's kitchen surpassed anything Merry had ever seen in a showroom. The cupboards lining the walls were polished mahogany, which glowed an amber hue. The counters were deep-blue quartz. One wall contained a carved mahogany bookcase and a commercial-sized wine cooler. On the other side of the bookcase stood another huge cooler filled with masses of cut flowers. The center of the room was commanded by a prep counter that boasted an inlaid wooden chopping board, a stainless steel cutting station, and a marble slab for baking. Overhead, the vaulted ceiling held racks of highly polished copper pots. The adjacent dining area was semicircular, with floor-to-ceiling French doors that opened out to the magnificent ocean view.

"Don't tell me you cook!" she said. "But you don't have a stove."

Barry smiled. "Go over to the bookcase and touch the door."

Merry did as instructed, and out slid a stove, wall ovens, and a sink. She was as delighted and surprised as a child seeing her first Christmas tree.

"I do it to relax," Barry said, as if he was embarrassed by all this opulence. "And when you live alone, you better know how to sustain yourself. How about an omelet with the coffee?"

"I think I'm off food until tomorrow. But I would like a rain check."

"A rain check it is. What about brunch on Sunday? We can eat outside on the terrace."

"Sunday isn't going to work for me. I have to go back to the city on Friday." Her voice conveyed her disappointment.

"Any chance of getting out of it?" He stood there with his hands in his pockets, looking like a little boy who had just learned that the circus was not coming to town.

"I don't know. Let's talk about it tomorrow. I'll find out if I can juggle some dates."

"Merry, there isn't someone else, is there?"

"My answer is the same as before—no, there isn't."
He nodded and started to prepare the coffee.

Something happened to Merry as she and Barry sat on
the terrace, drinking the excellent brew he had prepared.
She was beginning to have feelings for him that she had
never felt for Randy. There was no sparring or teasing,
and no glib comebacks entered her mind. She was feeling
an awakening of affection that could develop into more
with time.

"You're quiet. Can you share your thoughts?" he
asked.

She toyed with her coffee cup. "I'll share if you share."

"You go first. You're the guest."

"This is a bit difficult to put into words, but I feel
comfortable when I'm with you."

"Just comfortable?" He pulled his chair closer.

"No, not just comfortable, but... happy. And safe. I
feel safe when I'm with you, and I like that feeling."

"Nothing more?"

He smiled his dazzling smile. She noticed again, and
this time more closely, how handsome Barry was, with his
deep auburn hair, green eyes, and slight tan. But it was
the sound of his voice that she liked so much. It wasn't
one of those raspy, loud men's voices that had all the
charm of a public-address system.

"I've told you enough," she said. "Now it's your turn."

"Let's see... I'm falling for you. I think we should
take it slow, but not take forever to make up our minds.
We should get to know each other better, and that will
take some time. A lifetime, I hope." He kissed her on the
cheek. "Okay, it's your turn again."

"Well, I wasn't expecting to hear all that," she whispered.

"But you haven't told me what you think."

She took her time answering. "What do I think? I think I'd like to see what happens. Is that what you want me to say?"

"I want you to say what you mean, not what you think I want to hear."

"Then I'll say I agree with you. But I don't think it. I know it." She blinked tears from her eyes.

He smiled again. "Was that so hard? Now finish your coffee, and I'll take you home. Then you can check on the weekend. I would like you to stay."

"So would I. I'll change my plans first thing in the morning."

He leaned over and kissed her. It was the kind of kiss Merry wished would last forever.

Thirty-Five

January 1995

When Merry awoke, her first move was to reach for the phone to call Randy and tell him she was not returning on Friday.

"Randy, it's Merry." The determination in her voice matched her resolve.

"Hi, kiddo, what's going on?"

In a rush of words, she told him that she could not come to New York on Friday.

"Merry, you know I'm expecting you. Why the last-minute change?"

"I couldn't change an appointment with the building inspectors. It's easier to get an appointment with a brain surgeon. But you'll be pleased to know that the house is going to be finished earlier than anticipated."

"Is that what you called to tell me? Merry, after the other night, I thought you would want to come back."

"Aren't you forgetting an important aspect of your life? Aren't you engaged?"

"That's what I want to talk about. I owe you an explanation about this whole thing. But I want to do it when you're here."

"Why can't it wait a week? Whatever you want to say won't get stale."

"Look, if you can't come here, I'll fly down there today. I'll let you know when my flight's supposed to get in, and you can pick me up at the airport."

She was silent.

"Merry, are you there?"

"Yes, I'm here, but I don't understand what's so urgent that you have to fly down now. What are you up to?"

"No twenty questions, kiddo. Just humor me, okay?"

"Okay, why not? Let me know your flight, and I'll meet you at the airport."

What was that all about? she wondered as she hung up. Had Randy decided to stop work on the house and sell it? Maybe he'd lost all his money and couldn't afford beach towels. Whatever the reason for his sudden return, she detected a storm blowing in from the north.

For the first time, Merry knew that she wanted to get on with her life in whatever way it would play out. But there was one thing she did not want—and that was to continue her relationship with Randy Grant. When the house was finished, so was she. But how was she going to tell him?

The ringing of the telephone interrupted her excursion into this realm of thought.

"Merry?"

"Barry, hi. I had a nice time last night. It really was lovely."

"That's why I'm calling. Have you canceled your weekend plans yet?"

"I'll know later on this afternoon. I just have some loose ends to tie up."

"Merry, does this have something to do with Randy Grant?"

"He's flying here this afternoon because I'm not going to fly up there."

"This doesn't change anything with us, does it?"

"No, of course not. When I said I agreed with you, I meant it. Especially the part about taking everything the way we discussed it. Why? Are you having second thoughts?"

"The only thoughts I have are that I want to see you this weekend."

"Persistent devil, aren't you?"

"You should only know. How about going out on the boat Saturday?"

"In Nassau?"

"I brought the boat back. It's at the yacht basin in West Palm. Nell and Holt can come along as chaperones, if you like."

"Why? Don't you trust me?"

"The more I get to know you, the more I like. You've got a great sense of humor—just don't take us as a joke."

"How could I?"

"Good. Are you working this morning?"

"Actually, no. I was planning to go out and get some coffee."

"Can you be ready in twenty minutes? I'll pick you up and make breakfast for you here."

"Then I'd better get going."

"How about fifteen minutes, then?"

"You got it."

At ten o'clock, Merry went down to the lobby to wait for Barry. Much to her surprise, he was already there.

"How did you get here so fast?"

"I was in the car when I called you. Let's go. I'm going to fill you with omelets."

"I have the distinct feeling this is going to be a very fattening relationship."

The Excalibur was gleaming in the sunshine. When Barry opened the door for Merry, she found a slim, square orange box tied with brown ribbon on the passenger seat. "Open it. This one's for you."

Merry carefully untied the ribbon, opened the box, and read the card resting on the tissue. *You sailed into my life. Stay anchored.* Under the tissue, she unfolded a silk scarf with a nautical motif.

"I love it," she said. "I've never had a Hermès scarf. It's almost too nice to wear. Thank you." She leaned over and kissed him.

"You'd better put it on or your hair will get wind-blown."

She wrapped the scarf around her hair. The silk felt as soft as a caress.

In the daylight, she compared Barry's home to Randy's. Barry's had a charm that was absent in Randy's. Here, there was comfort and elegance and, best of all, a feeling of seclusion that was missing in Randy's open structure.

"I hope you're hungry," Barry said, "because I'm prepared to outdo myself."

"Keep this up, and I'll hire you as my cook."

"I accept the job."

She followed him into the kitchen, but he suggested she take a look around the house while he got breakfast ready.

"Can't I do something? I'm really not all that help-less."

"I'm trying to impress you, so please humor me."

Merry wandered from room to room, discovering the real Barry through framed pictures of family and friends, diplomas, awards, and trophies for golfing, tennis, and yachting. Books lined the shelves of his mahogany-pan-eled library. Seascape paintings blended into each of the eight rooms, and she had never seen bathrooms so luxu-

riously outfitted—all six of them. Fireplaces of carved
marble stood in the bedrooms, library, and living room.

She stepped out onto the terrace and discovered,
behind a wall of tall ficus, a five-room guesthouse with
light bamboo floors and whitewashed, pecky cypress walls.
In the main room, tropical-patterned bark cloth in soft
tones of green and peach covered two bleached-wicker
sofas and the deep club chairs. French doors opened to
a dazzling spread of white beach that led to the ocean.

Beyond the guesthouse, she discovered a Key West-
style building that contained apartments for Barry's staff
of housekeeper, chauffeur, and groundskeeper. And
framed by palm trees and blooming vines of bougainvillea was the five-car garage. *This,* she thought with a
sigh, *is a self-contained paradise.*

When she returned to the house, she found the
housekeeper setting the table on the terrace. Barry was
sitting on a chaise longue, drinking coffee.

"So what do you think?" he asked. "Do you like my
single-guy attempt at playing house?"

"I love it. It's charming. I'll take it."

"I was hoping you'd say that. I want you to like it. Sit
next to me."

She sat next to him on the wide chaise longue as he
motioned to the housekeeper to bring another cup of
coffee.

"I'd like to know more about you," he said. "Any
crimes you might have committed—that sort of thing."

"Where shall I start? I was born in Kerry Lakes, New
Hampshire, and graduated from high school there.
Worked in the furniture field since I was fourteen. Got
a job at La Viola in Boston. Got my decorator's certification and came to New York when I was twenty-nine. I've
managed the same studio since then. My parents married
young. Mom's a waitress, and my dad works in the local

hardware store. One more thing—I lost my virginity two days ago."

He looked at her with his green eyes reflecting the ocean. "Fine. You're hired." They both laughed.

"Does this weekend have anything to do with Randy Grant?" he asked again. "I don't want to play games with you, and I don't want you to play games, either."

"I'm not." She paused as she gathered her thoughts. "Randy and I have known each other for years, and for years we were great at sparring with each other. Over those years, we would go out for drinks or dinner, just as friends. For a long time, I imagined I had feelings for him but never could express them, and I hoped he might have feelings for me too. Yet the thought of having that as a reality frightened me. I still don't understand why, except down deep, I didn't want the fantasy to become a reality. I know that now." As she spoke, Merry was talking to herself, about the person she once was.

"Can you tell me what happened two days ago?" Barry spoke in almost a whisper, as if his voice had hands about to pick up a wounded bird.

Tears welled in Merry's eyes. She couldn't speak, and she sat frozen on the edge of the chair.

"I didn't mean to upset you," Barry said. "Look, at our ages, you didn't really expect either of us to have lived celibate lives."

"But I did lead a celibate life," she said quietly. "Until," she paused and took a breath, "until two days ago."

He gently embraced her. "Come on. No one's running away here. You've got to know that. I'm in love with you, Merry. You're a wonderful girl—woman. Whatever you are, consider yourself mine."

"I love you too. You're actually the first person I have ever loved, and I want to be yours."

"It was Randy, wasn't it?"

"Yes, it was. He and I were working—or at least that's what I thought we were doing—when it all happened. I did nothing to stop it. It was my first time. I didn't know what to expect. I know now I should have had more self-control, but I wasn't thinking. Not even about the fact that Randy is engaged. Everything came together so fast."

"Things happen. You probably were lonely. Everyone gets lonely. I've been lonely too. But not anymore, and you shouldn't be either. I want to love a woman, not a child." Barry paused for a moment. Merry started to speak, but he put his hand out to stop her from going on. "Let me finish. We're not kids. If we don't know what we want now, we never will. We don't have the luxury of all the time in the world. This is our now—it won't be like this for either of us ever again."

"Barry, is this really it for us. Are we—?"

"Yes we are. This is what we both want."

Merry whispered, "Oh yes, Barry. This what we both want—to be together forever."

"Was that so hard?" Barry said as he gave her a knowing look. His mood changed. He looked deeply into her eyes. "So what are you going to do about Randy?"

"I'll meet him at the airport this afternoon, tell him about us, and send him back to Elizabeth."

"Good girl. We're going to the airport together." He embraced her and said, "Let's eat breakfast, and then we'll go for a little shopping excursion."

Merry ate little of what Barry had prepared.

"Don't you like my cooking?"

"I can't eat. I can barely think."

"Well, a house could fall on me, and I think I'd still be hungry. Shall we go?"

"I'll go freshen up."

"That will give me time to make a call. But don't be too long. We've got things to do today."

"Yes, sir," Merry said as she headed down the hall.

Five minutes later, Barry called out, "Ready?"

"I just have to put on my scarf."

"Luis is going to drive the Shadow, so you won't need it." She put the scarf around her shoulders instead, and they left the house.

As they rode up South Ocean Boulevard, Barry told Luis to stop at Randy's unfinished house. Posted on the temporary fence that surrounded the property was a small For Sale sign. "Do you see that, Merry?"

"I know as much about it as you do. That's probably why Randy was so insistent about seeing me. I guess I won't know until I see him."

Luis continued on to Worth Avenue and stopped in front of Cartier. It was apparent the doorman was expecting them. He opened the car door for Merry, and Luis opened the door for Barry. Merry figured it was the typical morning pageant on Worth Avenue, and the tourists were staring.

"I bet they hire actors to make us think this kind of thing goes on all the time," commented one plump woman in polyester white slacks and an oversized tunic.

"You wanna take a picture of the car and the show-fooer?" her husband asked.

"Why not? The girls at home will love it. And by the way, it's pronounced *shoffore.*"

"How do you know how it's pronounced?"

"I read it in a book."

"Oh."

They took the photo and walked across the street.

Barry led Merry by the hand into the cool marble-and-glass treasure chest, Cartier. The place smelled of diamonds.

A dark-suited man greeted them. "Good morning, Mr. Chadwick. We were expecting you. What may we show you today?"

Barry looked at Merry. "Let's see some engagement rings, Sigmund." He put his arms around her and whispered, "This is my idea of taking it slow."

The only response Merry could muster was, "Oh?"

They were ushered into a small but elegantly furnished room that contained a loveseat pulled up to a highly polished ormolu-trimmed table. A tufted leather chair was on the other side of the table.

Sigmund pulled the loveseat out for Merry and Barry and sat in the leather chair. An associate entered, carrying a long black velvet box.

Sigmund instructed the man to place the box on the table and then to bring a bottle of champagne. Opening the box, he turned it to Merry and said, "Shall we get to work?"

Then everything went black.

"Merry, it's okay. Here, drink this water."

Finding herself half on the floor and being propped up by Barry, a confused and disoriented Merry choked out, "What happened?"

"You passed out. Are you all right?"

"Yes. It's just that I never saw anything like these in my life. It's positively overwhelming. I'm fine now. It just takes a bit of getting used to."

Barry propped her back on the love seat and whispered, "Pick any one you like."

Merry was speechless.

"All right, then I'll pick one." Barry selected a large emerald-cut stone set in a simple platinum ring, flanked by two baguettes. "What do you think of this one? Try it on." He slipped the ring on her finger.

"It's ten carats," Sigmund said, "but we can show you a larger stone if you like, Mr. Chadwick."

"Merry has to decide. What do you think? Do you like it?"

"I don't know what to say."

Barry was still holding her hand. "For starters, you could let me know if you like this ring."

"Oh, yes. It's so beautiful. I just love it."

"Mark it sold. Now, we'd like a little of that champagne, Sigmund."

Sigmund filled two Saint-Louis crystal champagne flutes with the nectar of celebration. "Congratulations to you and your intended, Mr. Chadwick. Now if you'll excuse me, I'll take care of the paperwork for you."

"Just send it to the office."

"Certainly, Mr. Chadwick."

"You've had quite a morning, haven't you, darling?" Barry hugged her.

"To say the least." Merry couldn't take her eyes off the pure white gem.

"Since I don't think you want to take your ring off, I'll just have to do this." Barry got down on one knee and, taking Merry's hand in his, said, "Merry, this is really for keeps. Will you marry me?"

"Oh, yes, yes. I will marry you."

"And when will this happen?"

"Not a year from now," Merry beamed.

"How about as soon as we get a license?" He put his arm around her.

"Then let's do it."

"We can go over to the West Palm Courthouse first thing tomorrow morning."

Merry was having a difficult time keeping her feet on the ground. She thought she was flying, but Barry had his arm around her, so she remained earthbound.

"Let's pick wedding and honeymoon dates over dinner tonight. Is that all right with you, Miss Venture?"

"I'd be delighted, Mr. Chadwick."

His kiss ignited her soul and seared away all vestiges of her haunting inner dialogues. At last she was free and truly in love—and truly loved.

By noon on Friday, they had the license and, with Luis driving, headed for the airport to meet Randy's plane. The mood changed. "I don't know what Randy's up to," Barry said, "but we both have contracts with him, so we'll meet him together."

"It would be a good idea. When I saw him, the house was very much on his mind. I don't have a clue about what's going on."

They went inside the terminal and waited for Randy to appear at the gate. Passengers filed out, looking sun-starved and anxious to get on with their winter respite. But there was no Randy.

"Maybe he took a later flight," Barry said.

A woman in a business suit and carrying a briefcase walked over to Merry as if she recognized her. "Are you Merry Venture?"

"Yes, I am."

"I'm Nancy from Mr. Grant's office. He wants you to have this." The woman handed a large manila envelope to Merry.

"Where is he now?" Merry asked.

"He couldn't make the flight, so he sent me down to meet you."

"Thank you. But how did you know who I am?"

"Mr. Grant showed me a photo." With that, Nancy excused herself to catch the return flight to New York.

"You can open it on the way home," Barry said as he steered Merry toward the exit.

As soon as they got in the car, Merry opened the envelope and found that there were two smaller ones inside.
Each one had a message typed on the outside: Read this
first. Read this second.

"What is this?" Barry asked. "Something out of *Alice in
Wonderland?*"

Merry opened the first envelope. It contained two
typewritten pages. She glanced at the end to see how it
was signed. Just Randy's name.

> Merry,
>
> You're probably wondering why I'm not
> on the flight. There was a complication,
> and I had to rebook the flight. I'm due
> in around five, and I'll meet you at your
> hotel.
>
> After I told you I was getting married,
> I realized I shouldn't have said anything
> until I was sure I was going to go through
> with it. It looks as if Elizabeth beat me to a
> decision. When she arrived here last week,
> things between us began to fall apart. Eliz-
> abeth admitted she doesn't want to live in
> the States. I don't want to live in England.
> It was all very civilized. She stayed in my
> apartment when I flew down to see you. I
> wanted to see if you and I had any chance
> to make a go of it. I thought we did, but
> your reluctance to fly up here made me
> realize it's probably too late for us.
>
> When I returned to the city, I found
> that Elizabeth had left me a farewell note
> with her engagement ring and had flown
> back to London. I should never have
> gotten involved with Elizabeth, but the
> time seemed right when I was over there.

I'm not sorry about what happened
between us. It just should have happened
years ago, but I wasn't ready for any kind of
commitment. That was my mistake.

Anyway, I was pretty upset with Elizabeth for stringing me along when you
and I could at least have started to know
each other in a more meaningful way. I'm
hoping you will give me another chance
and let me make everything up to you. I'm
willing to give it a try if you are.

If you like, we could spend the weekend
at the Four Seasons, talk things over, and
see where we're going.

'Til then,
Randy

"What do you make of this?" Merry asked and handed
the letter to Barry. "The guy has some ego," she said when
he was finished reading. "We were never together... ever."

"This guy is bad news. No real apology, just a long
harangue about how he feels. I knew him at MIT. A lot
of talent but a side of arrogance. He's still a brilliant but
spoiled brat."

"But he's not our brat," Merry said as she opened the
second envelope.

Merry,

I wanted you to read what I had to say
before I give you any explanation about
why I'm selling the house. First, I want you
to know that the contract I have with you will
be honored. I have sent a check to Reno

to cover your services. Barry and everyone
else will get payment as soon as the work is
completed.

When things went downhill with Elizabeth, I decided to put the house on the
market with Sotheby's. I called Danielle,
my broker at Sotheby's, and she told me
that all during construction, there had
been interest in the place by a party who
wanted to buy the property, even if it wasn't
completed. That was yesterday. Danielle
had the Palm Beach office put a sign up
in case it fell through. Just as I was ready
to leave my apartment for the airport, she
called with an offer to buy the place and
met me at the airport with a check in hand
and a signed contract. I made money on
the deal, so it worked out for the best.

Randy

Barry nodded as he finished the second letter. "As big
a jerk as this guy is, he's an honest businessman. That's
why we like doing business with him. Let's go. There's
something I want to show you. And don't spend any time
thinking about this guy. The house is sold. It's over."

"Thankfully. All I want to do is get on with our lives."

"Luis, we'll go to the yacht basin."

The ride was a jangle of afternoon traffic, but Luis
knew that no car would dare crowd the Shadow.

"We're almost there," Barry said. "Close your eyes,
Merry, and don't open them until I tell you. And no
cheating."

She covered her eyes with her hands. "Are you kidnapping me somewhere?"

"My fondest desire, but no, it's just an ordinary surprise."

"I've never heard of an ordinary surprise."

"You will. Now I'm going to lead you out of the car and guide you to where I want you to stand. Ready?"

"Do I have a choice?"

"Absolutely none."

Trusting him completely, Merry allowed Barry to lead her some distance away from the car. "Okay, now you can look."

"I don't believe it." She stood facing one of the largest yachts she had ever seen. And she had seen those only in magazines. "Barry, is this true?"

"If you can read, it is."

In bright letters made of brass, the name *Merry Venture* was secured to the port side of the sleek ocean-going craft.

"What do you think? And don't pass out on me again."

"Pass out? This could cause cardiac arrest."

"Care to board her?"

"Do we have time?"

"You can use the phone on the boat to call the hotel and tell Randy to meet us here."

Us. Meet us. I'm part of an "us" floated through Merry's overjoyed mind.

"If you want to freshen up, you can go to the powder room." Barry led her down a short flight of stairs. In the room, a small basket held linen hand towels imprinted with the boat's name, *Merry Venture.*

Merry looked into the mirror and saw a woman she didn't know. When she put her left hand on her right shoulder, her reflection was a portrait of a beautiful woman wearing an enormous diamond engagement ring.

Thirty-Six

January 1995

When Merry reappeared on deck, Barry handed her a flute of champagne. "Because you never really got to drink the one at Cartier. Passing out is a real waste of good champagne." Merry took the glass, and she and Barry touched goblets in a toast to their future. "I've been thinking," Barry continued, "that it would be better if we left a message for Randy to meet us at the Four Seasons. We can have a short meeting with him, and then we'll go pick up some things from the hotel for you, and go back to my place to get ready for the weekend. What do you think?"

"That's a good idea. There really isn't anything for me to say to him anymore. I'm glad you and I are doing this together. Should I call and leave the message now?"

"Might as well. We'll meet him at six thirty. That should be plenty of time for him to get out of the airport and check in at the hotel."

She called the Palm Crest Inn, intending to ask the desk clerk to leave the message for Randy. However, when she said her name, the woman who answered said she had a message for Merry.

"It arrived about an hour ago. Shall I read it to you?"

"Yes, please."

"It says, 'Kiddo, plans changed again. Will be on the flight landing at seven o'clock. See you at eight at your hotel. Nothing to worry about. Love, Randy.' Do you care to leave a message in case he calls again?"

"Can you hold on for a minute?" Merry told Barry what had happened and asked if they should go back to the Palm Crest Inn at eight to meet him.

Barry shook his head in disgust. "The hell with him. What makes you think he'll be on that flight either?"

Merry turned back to the phone. "No message. But thank you."

"Do you have a number where you can be reached?"

"Not at the moment. Thanks again." Merry handed the phone back to Barry.

"Come on," he said. "I'll give you a tour of the *Merry Venture.*"

It wasn't so much the size of the craft but the detail of the appointments that astonished Merry. It was a floating palace, complete with staterooms, salon, small library, large dining room, and a gleaming stainless-steel galley.

"I'm saving the best for last." Barry led her up a small flight of stairs on the top deck and opened a door. The enormous master stateroom was a suite of rooms containing his and her baths, two walk-in closets, and a dressing room—all in shades of peach and ivory. "Well, what do you think of it?"

"Who can think? So much has happened today, I can barely sort it all out. But to answer your question, it is wonderful."

He wrapped his arms around her and held her close. She could hear their hearts beating together. When he kissed her, she felt herself melting into his arms, becoming fused to him. They stood in the embrace, enjoying the closeness of each other.

Barry finally broke the silence. "We're going to do this the right way. This place is for our honeymoon."

"I was hoping you would say that. I want this to be right too. When we begin our lives together, I want it to be a real beginning."

"Me too." He kissed her again. And once again, she melted. "I think we'd better go now, if we want to save the moment."

"Couldn't agree more."

They left the boat and returned to the car. "Why don't you take your stuff out of the hotel and move it to our place now? You can call La Viola from home, and let him know you'll no longer be working for him. And invite him to come down for our wedding. What do you say?"

"I hadn't thought that far, but I will make the call." She looked into Barry's eyes with love and said, "'From home,' if that's what you'd like."

"I'd like it very much. So it's settled. Let's go back, and you can check out."

When Merry checked out of the hotel, she did not leave a forwarding address. All she said was that she'd call later to see if there were any messages.

When they entered Barry's house a short time later, Mrs. Adams greeted them. "Do you need anything, Mr. Chadwick?"

"Why don't you show Miss Venture to her room?"

Apparently, Mrs. Adams had been informed earlier which room was to be Merry's. "It's a lovely room. You'll like it."

"I know I will, Mrs. Adams."

The two women walked down a wide foyer. "This one is yours. Mr. Chadwick's room is next door." Merry entered a pale French blue and gray room; the bed had been turned down. An open door revealed a bathroom and a dressing room. "Can I get you anything?"

"I'm fine," Merry replied with an enormous smile.

Mrs. Adams said good night and closed the door, leaving Merry alone for the first time since ten that morning. How wonderful it felt to be quiet and excited at the same time. What she'd love right now, she decided, was to take a nice bath and to go to sleep. As long as she didn't wake up and discover this was all just a dream.

No sooner had she started her bath than the phone in her room rang. It was Barry. "Would you like to take a sunset walk on the beach later on? But first, let's have dinner on the patio. We can watch your ring sparkle in what's left of the sun."

"I'll meet you on the terrace in twenty minutes."

"Don't get lost."

"Don't worry; I won't." She hung up and then floated in her perfumed tub for a luxurious but all-too-short soak.

A mixture of heavy tropical air, sea spray, and the lapping of the tide against the shore added to the mystery of the starlit night. Merry and Barry were alone in what seemed like a universe of only them. The moon shimmered down on the water, leaving a silver path that stretched far out to the horizon.

"You're so deep in thought. Care to clue me in?" He kissed her on the neck and put his arm around her.

"Just thinking about today. Thinking about us, and everything that's happened, and how fast it all happened. My head's still spinning." She dug her feet into the cool sand and looked at Barry. He held her close as they walked along the deserted beach. "Care to share your thoughts?" she whispered.

He stopped walking and stood heart to heart with her. "I was thinking about our wedding plans. We have the license. Let's get married on Wednesday. That is, if you aren't busy that day." He hugged her even tighter.

"Where would we have the ceremony?"

"What about here? On Wednesday at sundown?"

"That sounds wonderful. I don't know anyone here to invite."

"Merry, you mean to tell me that you don't know Nell and Holt? They would never forgive us if we didn't have them stand up for us. And what about your friends in New York? You should call them, you know. And your parents. And don't forget Reno."

"I plan to call them all tomorrow. What about your parents?"

"I wish I could, but both of them died several years ago. My dad died in his sleep while they were on a cruise. The doctors said it was a stroke. He went to bed one night and never woke up."

"And your mother?"

"It was a tragedy. She and Dad were soul mates. She was never the same after he went. Within a year, she was gone. Everyone thought it was a broken heart, but the doctors said it was an inoperable brain tumor. Mom thought Dad didn't know, but he did, and I suspect that's what killed him. They were a great couple and loving parents. I loved them and still miss them. I know they would have loved you too, Merry."

"I'm so sorry. Now I miss them. Do you have any brothers or sisters?"

"Sort of. There's my younger brother, Wade."

"What do you mean, sort of?"

"Wade's two years younger than I am. It's funny; we grew up in the same family, with the same love and the same advantages. After he graduated from Yale, he got involved with an older woman. She was bad news—drinking, drugs. He had some money of his own, and most of it went up his nose and hers. He tried rehab a couple of times, but it never worked. Right after our mother died, I got a call from Seattle. Wade said he was trying to find himself. Apparently, he had left that playmate because he said he was living with a waitress. Then we heard nothing. About a year ago, Wade sent me a meandering letter, in a scrawl I could barely make out, telling me he was going to Europe. Probably Amsterdam, because of their liberal drug policies. I haven't heard from him since."

Barry was silent for a moment. Then he continued, "The past is over. We both have a wonderful future with each other, and that's all that counts. Maybe we should go in and make our honeymoon plans. Or are you too tired?"

"I'll force myself."

"Good girl." He kissed her on the forehead, and they headed back to the house.

Later, Barry said good night to Merry. "Get some sleep. We have a lifetime for everything else."

It was a wonderful, dreamless sleep, like floating on a cloud. When Merry awoke the next morning, she discovered Barry sitting on the chaise longue in her room, waiting for her to get up.

"Well, good morning, sleepyhead," he said. "Do you know what time it is?"

Like a contented cat, Merry stretched under the satin quilt. "Why? Are you giving a test?"

"No, but I'll get you breakfast in bed, if you like."

"Best offer I've had all day. And by the way, it's almost ten."

If this is the beginning of my new life, Merry told herself, *then I am the happiest woman in the world.* It didn't take her long to get ready for the day. She didn't want to waste a minute.

Thirty-Seven

January 1995

When Merry called her mother to tell her the good news, it was met with the predictable pessimism of a woman whose horizon for happiness was forever at an unattainable distance. Years of pent-up rage and the inability to feel or express warmth had successfully alienated mother and daughter, leaving only the skeletal remains of what might have been a family.

Every day, Glenda Venture lived out a routine, a performance in which she starred and directed. After a day of serving customers at the diner, she walked the few short blocks to her dilapidated home and prepared for her entrance into her evening drama. The costume was always the same: an old bathrobe, old slippers. Then Glenda perched on the end of the sofa, with her legs tucked up under her, with her bottle of scotch, her big ashtray, and the perpetual scowl that would remain until she returned to work the next day.

When the phone rang that Saturday, Glenda took her time in answering it. Why bother to rush? It was no doubt a call to change shifts with one of the girls.

"Hello?"

"Ma, it's Merry."

"Ya didn't lose yoah job, did ya?"

"No. Why would you think that?"

"That's good. The money ya send is a help."

"I'm glad. Listen, Ma, I have some news. I'm getting married."

"Oh, my God. Yoah not pregnant, ahr ya?"

"No, I finally met someone I really care about."

"Ahr ya supportin' him?"

"Of course not. Just called to tell you and Dad. I thought you might like to wish me happiness."

"Listen, missy, ya should know by now that ya make yoah own happiness. Nobody can wish happiness on a person. Ya get what ya get."

"Well, I just wanted to let you and Dad know."

"So when is this weddin'?"

"Next Wednesday."

"And yo'ah sure yo'ah not pregnant? Isn't this awful sudden? Nobody in ahr family ever had a bastid."

"Is that what you think? How could you even entertain such an ugly thought?"

"There ya go, on yo'ah high horse. All I said was—"

"I know what you said. I'll just pretend I didn't hear it. Why can't we ever have a nice mother-daughter conversation?"

"We ahr. Ahrn't we talkin' now?"

"I guess I should know by now how our talks go."

"If it will make ya feel any better, then I hope yo'ah happy."

"I have to go now. Don't forget to tell Dad, okay?"

"What do you think, I'm senile? Of course, I'll tell him. The ideas you come up with."

"Bye, Ma."

"Well, thanks for calling."

That was it. The duty call had been made. Merry walked out to the terrace to enjoy the early evening air.

Glenda resumed her place on the sofa and took a long drag before she ground her cigarette into a half-empty coffee cup. The ashtray had already fallen to the floor. "She cahn't fool me. She's in trouble." After her second scotch, Glenda turned on the television and fell asleep.

Doug no longer came home for supper but grabbed a beer and a pizza at Kerry Lakes' bowling alley. He had yet to perfect his score.

Thirty-Eight

July 1947–July 1951

The unintended pregnancy of little Glenda Armstrong came about from curiosity over a subject her mother refused to discuss with her. The Armstrong household was ruled by wife and mother, Margaret Alston Armstrong, and dutifully followed by husband and father, Wayne Timothy Armstrong. Certain words and questions were considered filthy by both parents and were rebuked by swift punishments, which were intended as deterrents for future queries. For Glenda, this became a game of just how much she could get away with by acting as if she didn't know what she was talking about, which in reality was true. What she did know about was schoolyard whispers and giggles.

With the face of an angel and her sweet voice, the eleven-year-old commenced on one of her questioning routines. "Ruthie Straw said that bastids are babies who don't have parents, but I said they're orphans. Who's right?"

It didn't take long for her mother to get all bug-eyed, with veins popping out on her forehead. Glenda thought this was very funny.

"And just when did this Ruth Straw tell you this?"

"Yesterday, on the way to school. Ruthie knows lots of things about—"

"Now you listen to me, young lady, you are not to associate with this bad influence. I am going to call Mrs. Straw and tell her I forbid her daughter to have anything more to do with you. Do you understand?"

"Please, Mummy. Ruthie will tell everyone at school that you did. Oh, please, Mummy, please."

"Then let this be a lesson to you. There will be no dirty talk in this house. Do you un-der-stand me, young lady? Now go to your room and do not come out until suppah."

Some of her mother's huffing and puffing subsided as she headed toward the living room, where her bottle of scotch stood on the upper shelf of the desk.

Glenda's bedroom was on the first floor in the back of the house, so it was easy for her to climb out the window, hop on her bike, and ride at breakneck speed to Ruthie's house to continue their illicit conversation.

By five thirty, Glenda was back in her room, pretending to study. In actuality, she was writing down all the words she and Ruthie decided to share with everyone at recess the following day. Glenda would write the first ten, and Ruthie would provide the explanations.

"Glenda," her mother called in her shrill voice. "I been calling you for the last fi' min'ts. Din' you hear me?"

Two stiff scotches had left Mrs. Armstrong a bit woozy.

"I didn't heah you," Glenda said. "I'm studyin' for the test tomorrow." She shoved the list under her desk blotter.

"Suppa's in fi' min'ts. Go wash up."

And that was that, or so it seemed.

By the time Glenda was thirteen, her mother's "nerves" had taken a turn for the worse and she had to go away for a few weeks' rest. Glenda stayed with her grandparents. During that time, Glenda began to mature, and, bewildered, she sought Ruthie's reliable counsel. Ruthie knew so much about "stuff," and her source of information was impeccable. Her brother Billy, who was tall for his age at twelve, was a Boy Scout with badges in camping, archery, and citizenship. Some of the stuff Billy told Ruthie didn't make sense, according to Ruthie, but at least it gave her and Glenda a general idea about what boys and girls did together. But really, it was so stupid.

How could something like that work?

A month later, Mrs. Armstrong returned with new resolve to be calm, and to take a nap every afternoon, and not to go to the shelf in the living room desk. Upon a just-to-see inspection, she found that the entire shelf had been emptied of its bottles. *Keep calm*, she told herself as she hurried toward her bedroom. There on her dressing room table was her reserve stash, visible to all, in her collection of large drugstore perfume bottles. One little swig and then she'd take her nap. Dinner would be hot dogs and beans.

Time moved on, and Glenda reached her fourteenth birthday, which would not be celebrated because of her big mouth. Both parents agreed that rudeness at the dinner table would not be tolerated. All she had said was that eating baked beans three times a week gave her gas. It wasn't like she'd said *fart*.

With her birthday approaching and knowing that there would be no party or presents, Glenda and Ruthie decided it would be fun to have a party on their own and to ask some girls and some cute boys for a picnic. The event would take place in the abandoned barn behind Ruthie's house. They would have peanut butter sandwiches, brownies, and lemonade, and a cake Ruthie said her mother would bake. Now, this was going to be fun. All they had to do was invite the usual girlfriends and some boys. Glenda would invite Dougie Venture.

Dougie Venture was one of the cute boys. He was fifteen and considered the dumbest kid in grammar school and high school. His greatest ambition was to have a high bowling score. But he was fun and always laughed at everything Glenda said. Sometimes on Saturdays, they would go for bike rides and talk and laugh about nothing in particular, which for Glenda was just about the only attention and warmth she ever got. And he was cute, with a tousled thatch of black hair and gray-blue eyes, though he was not particularly tall. And with his shyness, and because he was one of the "shop" kids taking manual training classes, Dougie didn't stand a chance with the popular kids. But Glenda wasn't one either. Her friends were the same ones from grade school who the popular kids considered to be daredevils.

One Saturday during the summer, when Glenda and Dougie were walking along the railroad tracks, they decided to have what they thought was an adult conversation. After all, they were almost adults—Glenda, now fourteen and a half, and Dougie, fifteen and a quarter.

"So what should we talk about?" Dougie asked as he kicked a pebble that, in true Dougie style, didn't go very far.

"I thought ya knew what adults talk about," Glenda said, disappointed.

"Well, I do know that my parents always argue about bills, but I don't have any, so I guess we can't talk about that." He stooped to pick up another pebble.

"All my parents do is argue about my mother's nerves and how expensive it is for her to go away and rest. It's not like they're poor or anything. I mean, Dad's the vice president at the Kerry Lakes Savings Bank." Glenda decided that adult talk was boring. "I know, let's talk about the things Ruthie said her brother told her."

Clueless and blank-faced, Dougie replied, "What was that?"

"Well, she knows how babies are made."

Now Dougie was at full attention. "How does she know?"

"Her brother Billy is a Boy Scout, and he knows just about everything."

"Then what did she say?"

"Ya won't believe what she said. It's so dumb. We both couldn't stop laughing."

As the afternoon wore on, they exhausted their limited topics of conversation and decided to go to Dougie's house, eat watermelon, and see who could spit the seeds the farthest. After two big slices of melon, the fun of that activity was worn out. What to do next on that late-summer afternoon became the next topic.

Dougie suggested they take a look at his father's new flatbed truck, parked beside the garage next to the toolshed. "Bet Dad'll bust a gut if he finds out I was foolin' around with his pride and joy."

Dougie opened the door to the cab and, much to his surprise, found the keys on the seat. "Let's go for a ride out to the pond. My folks won't be back from work until at least seven tonight."

"But ya don't have a license."

"I take it out all the time to go fishin', and they don't even know. This will be fun."

Fun. Glenda's favorite word, especially when there was some danger involved. "Okay, but I gotta be home before six."

What a joy ride it was. A ride through the backwoods to Stone's Pond. With Dougie driving, and Glenda standing up in the bed in back, this sure was better than "adult talk." No sooner had Dougie parked under a stand of white pines than Glenda yelled out that this was so much fun, and guess what? She had found a bottle of orangeade and a blanket in the toolbox. A picnic!

They sat on the blanket and took turns drinking the soda. It then occurred to Glenda that they could resume their conversation about Ruthie's brother's information.

"I don't think her brother knows what he's talking about," she said, "but Ruthie doesn't make stuff up, even though she said the whole thing sounds stupid. And then Ruthie said the first time doesn't count because you don't even know if you'll like it."

"I heard that, too, from some of the football players talking about it in gym. Don't forget—they should know."

A silence fell over them as they considered what to do next. Glenda spoke first. "If we just experimented, then it really wouldn't be for real anyway."

After a moment's consideration, Dougie reasoned that finding something out was a good thing for when you really had to know, like when people got married. Babies could come only from married people. His father had told him that.

Awkwardly, with closed eyes, they fumbled and squirmed around until they thought they were doing "it." What was so special about that? And Ruthie's brother never said it was uncomfortable. How stupid. When she got home, she would call Ruthie and tell her the whole thing.

Three months later, after many days of Glenda feeling sick to her stomach, Mrs. Armstrong took her to the family doctor, where they learned the worst possible news. It was beyond Glenda's imagination as to how this could have happened. But the worst was still to come.

That night, a remarkably sober Margaret Armstrong told Wayne Armstrong the news of the day. His swift response was to remove his belt and beat the hapless child on her back and legs. In a state of shock, Glenda fell and, with great retching, threw up on the carpet. Mrs. Armstrong looked at the carpet, which had just been cleaned, and in a voice of controlled coldness demanded that Glenda clean up the mess. The last word Glenda heard as her parents exited the living room was "Disgusting."

Within the week, the fate of the two children was orchestrated by both sets of unhappy parents. Margaret and Wayne Armstrong and Anita and Ogden Venture were quick to blame the other, glaring and posturing until mutually exhausted. Wayne Armstrong finally broke the stalemate with a softening offer.

"Look, this is getting us nowhere. We need a plan. We need a drink."

He opened the desk and placed the new scotch bottle on the coffee table. Margaret ran to the kitchen to fetch the glasses and the always filled-and-ready ice bucket. Now, the problem would be solved.

The first drink was consumed in silence. The refill brought the plan. The third brought mutual condolences. What a disappointment those two kids were. The women cried; the men paced. Then Margaret broke the anguish of the moment. "I'll heat up some hot dogs and beans." It would be the fourth time that week Wayne ingested this delight. Dessert was another scotch.

The two sets of parents agreed that both Glenda and Dougie would be sent to live with respective grandparents, even though both sets lived in the same town. One was on the north side and the other on the south, which created a separation of three miles. Margaret Armstrong had already made arrangements to visit her sister in Vermont, leaving Mrs. Venture to face humiliation alone while working behind the counter at the local yard goods store. Secretly, Mr. Venture thought his son must be quite a guy.

A justice of the peace united Glenda and Dougie as husband and wife in the Ventures' living room. The bride did not carry a bouquet of stephanotis and lilies of the valley but a large handkerchief into which copious tears were shed. Dougie just stood there with his usual I-don't-get-it expression.

After the ceremony, Wayne Armstrong and Dougie's parents and the newlyweds convened in the kitchen for a breakfast of scrambled eggs, toast, and coffee. Mrs. Margaret Armstrong was not in attendance; she was away, "resting." Immediately following the repast, Glenda and Dougie were driven to the small converted garage, a gift from both sets of parents, that would be their home.

The garage had once been a storage shed for Cushman's Grocery Store on Railroad Street. Cushman was only too happy to sell the place, since he couldn't afford to pay the taxes. Mr. Armstrong hired a handyman who installed a bathroom, kitchen, electricity, and running water. When the project was completed, the garage had become a small but adequate four-room cottage. The furnishings from the attics of both sets of grandparents and the Ventures consisted of a kitchen table and four chairs, a bed, one dresser, two nightstands, a crib and changing table, three mismatched lamps, two living room chairs, a sofa, one mattress, and a pile of assorted pillows, sheets, and blankets. Wayne Armstrong, in a moment of parental conscience, gave the couple a set of dishes, pots and pans, and the rest of the kitchen furnishings that he knew full well his wife would never miss.

Thirty-Nine

January 1995

Gloria, Cappy, Shellie, Reno? Merry decided to call Gloria first with the good news.

"Gloria? Merry." Her voice was almost quivering with excitement.

"Merry, great hearing from you, but I'm practically out the door. I'm off to England for my big handbag trunk show at Harrods. Is everything all right?" Gloria sounded as if she actually had her foot out the door and hadn't a minute to carry on a lengthy conversation.

"Better than all right. I'm getting married on Wednesday, and—"

Gloria cut her off with a high-school-girl scream. "You're what? Really? Who is he? When did all this happen? Tell me. I can take a later cab. Married? Oh, Merry, tell Mama all."

"I met Barry, Barry Chadwick, through Randy. Can you believe it? Barry is a general contractor and builder and is overseeing Randy's place down here. It's not even finished, and Randy sold it."

"Who cares about Randy? Tell me more about Barry. This is an almost-too-good-to-be-true story. I'm so happy for you."

"I met him the day after I got down here, and neither of us had much to say to each other but to talk about the project. We'd go out for what I thought were business lunches and dinners, but things went so fast, it made my head spin. And he is so good-looking."

"Please don't tell me he wants to be a writer." Gloria's voice carried the sting of bitter disappointment of her failed marriage.

"Nothing like that. He's more of a workaholic, and that suits me. He's a regular guy who loves me, and sometimes I can't believe it."

"Oh, Merry, now that you are moving on, believe your happiness. Anyway, for my wedding present to you, I'm giving you the Big Success Tote, in Envy Me Green Alligator. It's from my latest Glad Sacques Collection, Don't Carry a Grudge. The bags start at five thousand dollars. Yours goes for—can you believe it?—seven thousands five hundred! Just call the office and give them your new address. Kiss, kiss. I need to find a taxi. I'm off to my new destiny."

Three more calls, Merry thought as she dialed Cappy.

"Cappy, it's Merry."

"Okay, so tell me something good. Is he rich and an orphan?"

"How did you know?"

"Why call? To get a New York weather report? Are you a couple, or what?"

"We're getting married on Wednesday."

"Oh, my God, the eternal virgin is finally opening the vestal gates. Good for you. So tell."

"Cappy, he's wonderful, totally single, and yes, he's an orphan. And just to satisfy you, he's rich."

"No, it's to satisfy you, and about time. I wish I could be there to see all this happen." Then, in true Cappy style, she changed the subject to Cappy. "Are you ready for this? The success of *Zee Zee* magazine has made it possible for Tyler and me to close on our dream house in the Hamptons. So, Merry, mansion dreams come true. We're both lucky, huh?"

"I guess... no, I know so," Merry replied. "At last I feel that I'm marching in the parade of life, not just sitting on the curbstone watching. Well, I have a million things to do, so I'll say bye for now."

"And hello to your new life, dear Merry. Got to go. My life's calling too."

Merry looked at her engagement diamond as she dialed Shellie's number. The pure white stone caught the light and sent a myriad of brilliant rainbow colors dancing before her eyes. As she listened to the phone ring, she imagined the colors were the diaphanous dresses of tiny fairies, leaping in a celebration dance of joy for her happiness.

"This is Amy Aldrich," a woman's voice answered in an obviously recorded message, "Vice President Shellie Hughes's secretary. Ms. Hughes will be out of the office until the end of the month. If you wish to reach her, please leave a message at our Zurich office by pressing pound, then seven."

Well, Merry thought, *that was quick and easy.* It looked like Mrs. Chadwick would contact VP Hughes at the end of the month.

She hung up, and the thought raced through her head that in all the years she'd known Gloria, Cappy, and Shellie, not once had she ever really had anything significant to say. They called her with news of their lives. When she called them, it always was about something they had ordered from her.

She finished with a call to Reno with her news. As soon as he heard her voice, he knew something was up.

"Dear heart, don't tell me you need an extension on the project." His voice carried a tongue-in-cheek lilt. "I get the feeling you have something to say. Am I right?"

"You are. You definitely are. Reno, I'm getting married on Wednesday."

"My suspicion was correct. Is it Randy?"

"It's Barry Chadwick."

"Thank God for big favors. Merry, I'm so happy for you. I know Barry. His company has done some construction work for us. I'd like to hear about everything, but it will have to wait until I get down to Florida sometime in June. I'm looking for a property in Palm Beach. Do you know a good decorator?"

She laughed. "What do you think? So until you get down here, I'll say, 'til then."

The conversations, all short and sweet, became the finale to the aria of loneliness and longing Merry had sung for so long, but now, no more.

Forty

January 1995

Nell and Holt insisted that the future Mr. and Mrs. Chadwick join them for sunset cocktails. When Merry and Barry got there, they found a surprise engagement party waiting for them. That ended their plans for spending time on the boat.

On Sunday, the celebration continued at The Breakers, where Merry and Barry hosted a brunch in a private dining room. Everyone from the Saturday party attended.

It was almost dusk when they returned to the house. The wedding train had definitely left the station.

"I bet Randy never showed up," Barry said abruptly.

"You're right. If it was so important, he would have gotten in touch with me."

"Now, can we get on with our lives, Mrs. Chadwick-to-be?"

"Say that again. I like the sound of it."

"I don't feel like talking, but I will kiss you."

"Nobody's stopping you, Mr. Chadwick."

Monday morning sped by, filled with wedding plans, and by noon Merry and Barry had arranged for a justice of the peace and had asked Nell and Holt to stand up for them. For Merry, it was a time in her life when thoughts of doom and disappointment did not consume her. She allowed herself to accept the flow of events that were changing her life in ways she could never have dreamed. This was her safe harbor. Barry, with his love, had rescued her from wallowing in her quicksand of self-destruction.

Nell stopped by early Tuesday morning. It was another sun-drenched day in paradise. "I'll take care of everything for the wedding supper," she told Merry. "Holt and I want to do this as our gift to you and Barry—and don't say no because I have already ordered a very special menu. Not to mention that Chef Andre will have a fit if he gets a cancellation. And I've ordered a to-die-for wedding cake."

Tears of joy filled Merry's eyes. "What can I say? This is wonderful. Barry and I more than appreciate all this. Nell, I don't know how I can ever say thank you enough."

"Think nothing of it. But remember, you owe me some volunteer time for my next event."

"Anything you want, Nell."

"That's nice." Nell smiled. "I'll remember that."

"Talk about blackmail."

"Aha, welcome to Palm Beach."

Merry handed Nell a cup of coffee. "To you, Nell."

Nell responded by putting her arm around Merry. "And to you too, my new partner in crime."

They both laughed.

By day's end, all the preparations for the wedding were completed. Barry planned the honeymoon cruise with the crew, while Merry purchased her long-awaited trousseau. When she returned, Barry was waiting for her on the terrace.

"It looks as if someone had a good time keeping Saks from going out of business." He walked over and kissed Merry before she had a chance to drop her packages.

"May I go out and come in again?" she said. "That was some kiss."

"For starters." He kissed her again. "My office called a few minutes ago. We got a check from Randy's firm for the completion of the house. He wants me to double the workers and get it done ASAP. And he left a message that he wants me to call him."

"Did you?"

"I'll call him at home tonight."

"What do you think he wants?"

"Your guess is as good as mine."

The phone rang. Mrs. Adams came out to tell Barry it was for him and took Merry's packages to her room. Merry decided to sit on the terrace for a while, but the while stretched out over half an hour. When Barry returned, he looked more annoyed than angry.

"It was Randy Grant. Can you believe that guy? He asked me if I knew where you were, and when I told him you were with me, he went nuts."

"You told him about us, I hope."

"I did, and he started shouting that the two of you had an understanding and that I had no right to interfere. Then I asked him why, if you two had an understanding, did he keep postponing his flight? Listen to this. He told me he had to think things over to be sure, and he couldn't make up his mind until it was too late to catch the last flight he said he'd be on. Merry, you would have been sitting there all night waiting for him to show up."

"So why call at all?"

"That's the craziest part. He wanted to know if I was really sure about you and me, because he'd like another chance with you. I told him I fell for you when I first met you, but I didn't know if you were involved with anyone else."

Merry laughed. "I didn't know I was involved. All this time, Randy was telling me he was getting married."

"You know what he said? 'Maybe I should have married Merry when I had the chance.'"

"I hate to disappoint him, but there was never a chance between us. I can see now that he's just a spoiled child. I want to forget about him."

"He plans to fly down on Friday. He'll have to be a pretty good swimmer to catch up with us."

"Then you didn't tell him about our getting married on Wednesday?"

"Let him read about it in the newspapers."

"And where do you plan to publish this news? In the *Shanghai Bugle*?"

"Among others."

They laughed and suddenly were in each other's arms.

For a moment after the kiss, the mood changed, and Barry looked into Merry's eyes. "You know, this house is as much yours as mine."

"After Wednesday, if I still like it." She paused, collected her thoughts, and went on. "There is one thing you haven't discussed with me, and I'm wondering…"

"If I want you to sign a prenuptial agreement? No, I don't, and I wouldn't consider it. This is the only marriage I will ever have. I love you unconditionally, and that's it. And while we're on the subject, I spoke with my lawyer this afternoon. I'm changing my will to put the house in your name along with mine. Now, can we talk about something else? Like what to do about dinner?"

Nothing tasted as good as a pizza when it was eaten in the kitchen, right out of the box. Add a glass of red wine, and it was a banquet. When the pizza was delivered, Barry gave the driver a big tip and ordered three more that could be frozen and sent to the boat early Thursday morning.

It was a silent supper, enhanced with the bottle of wine. There was nothing to say. All there was to do was enjoy each other's company. When they were done, Barry said, "Do you mind if I turn in and ignore you tonight, almost-Mrs. Chadwick?"

"So I'm boring you already?" She reached for his hand. "I'm so tired from all this running around that I'd like to get some rest myself."

"We can leave this for Mrs. Adams. Come on; I'll walk you home."

As he got up, he stumbled.

"Barry, what happened? Are you all right?"

"I don't know. All of a sudden, I've got this terrible headache. I think the wine got to me. I'll feel better in the morning."

"Why don't you stay with me? I'm worried."

"Because a glass of wine went to my head? Did you ever think I might be a nervous bridegroom?"

"But I'm worried, all the same."

"Then I'd like it if I could stay with you. I don't want you to think I'm just saying this to lure you into my clutches—but it might not be a bad idea."

"If it will make you feel better, then stay with me."

"I don't want to rush you. But you know how much I love you."

"As much as I love you."

"I'll be right back."

As Barry started down the hall to his room, he stumbled again. Merry rushed to him and propped him up against the wall. "We should get a doctor over here. You look so flushed! Where's his number? I'll call him."

"All those numbers are in the address book on my desk in the library. Merry, please help me to my room. My head is splitting."

Merry sat with Mrs. Adams and Luis in the library while Dr. Hugh Van Allen examined Barry in his bedroom. The waiting seemed to go on forever. When Dr. Van Allen came out of the bedroom, he summoned Merry before she had the chance to ask him what had happened.

"I'd like to talk to you privately, Miss Venture." When they were out of earshot of the staff, he continued. "I'd like to run a few tests on Mr. Chadwick, just to make certain everything is all right. Can you get him to the hospital now? I'll call the emergency room to expect him."

"Luis will drive us. What's the matter?" Merry was shaking and at the point of tears.

"I'm really not sure. I don't think it's anything to get alarmed about. But just to be safe, I'll call ahead."

When Merry went into Barry's room, he was sprawled on the bed with his hands over his eyes. "Barry, we're going to take you to the hospital for some tests. Dr. Van Allen just wants to be sure you're okay. Can you sit up?"

"I'm sorry about this, Merry. But nothing is going to stop our wedding plans."

"Of course nothing is going to stop them. Why even think such a thing? Luis is going to help you to the car, and I'll be with you all the time."

Merry could only think about not falling apart and was determined not to let Barry see her fear. She felt as if she were watching something happen that wasn't real.

Luis was there immediately, and he helped Barry outside to the Shadow. "You sit up here with me," he told Merry, "and let Mr. Chadwick lie down in the back."

"Is that okay with you, Barry, dear?"

As she spoke, Barry climbed into the backseat and stretched across it. By the time they got to the hospital, he was asleep.

The moment the Shadow pulled up, the emergency staff rushed out and put Barry in a wheelchair. Then the nightmare began.

For three hours, Merry and Luis sat in the hallway, waiting to hear from Dr. Van Allen. When he appeared, he was with another doctor.

"Miss Venture, this is Dr. Sajat Singh, a neurologist. He's going to explain what's going on."

Merry froze in her seat. She couldn't move.

"I've examined Mr. Chadwick," Dr. Singh said, "and we'd like to keep him overnight. We ran some tests, and we'll know more in the morning." He must have seen the terror in Merry's eyes, for he added, "If there was anything to worry about, I'd tell you. But I don't think there is. All we want to do is be on the safe side. Please don't worry. Go home and go to bed. I'll call you first thing tomorrow morning. Would you like something to help you sleep?"

"I don't think so, but thank you." A torrent of tears poured from her eyes. "Please tell me, is Barry going to be all right? Tell me it's not anything serious."

"We want him here so we can monitor him, but I don't think you need to worry. I promise you, you'll hear from me first thing in the morning. I'll say good night now."

"Good night, Doctor, and thank you. Luis, we should go now."

Merry spent a fitful night of constant anguish and intermittent dozing. At eight in the morning, Mrs. Adams woke Merry for the phone call. "Hello?"

"Dr. Singh here."

"Is Barry all right?"

"You can pick him up at ten. I'll see you both then."

"Yes."

Merry hung up and raced into the bathroom to get dressed. As she was brushing her teeth, she looked in the mirror. Overnight, she had aged. *My only chance at love. The only person I've ever really loved is Barry, and now something terrible is happening. How could things go on so perfectly? What kind of a dream world did I enter? Did I really think this happiness could go on forever? I'd be happy to live on Railroad Street with him for the rest of my life, if only he could be all right. Barry, don't be sick, please, don't be.* The torrent of tears opened again and gushed from her sad red eyes.

Pull yourself together, she thought. *This is not about you.*

She went to the kitchen to ring for Luis, but he was already there with a small travel case that he explained Mrs. Adams had packed with a change of clothes for Barry. He asked if she wanted to have a cup of coffee first, but she said she just wanted to go.

When they got to the hospital, Dr. Singh was waiting for her and suggested they talk in his office.

Chilled and dizzy, Merry felt like a zombie as she followed Dr. Singh. Barry was already in the doctor's office. When he saw her, he got up and kissed her and then they sat down together on the sofa as Dr. Singh sat behind his desk.

"As I suspected," the doctor said, "there isn't anything to worry about at the present. Just go about your normal plans, but take it easy. Stop rushing around so much. And I'd like you to stay in town for a week and set up an appointment to see me again at that time."

"Nothing to worry about?" Barry said. "That means you didn't find anything wrong with me?"

"Let's see how you do for a week. If you get any head-aches, I want you to call me right away, but as I said, this is all precautionary."

"We're getting married today."

"Congratulations. Get married. There is no reason why you shouldn't."

Barry laughed. Merry just sat there, still in a stupor.

"Well, I have to be going now," Dr. Singh said. "Once again, congratulations." He shook their hands and left.

Forty-One

January 1995

On the way home, Barry and Merry sat with their arms wrapped around each other.

"I want us to follow through on our plans and get married today," Barry said, "I want us to start our lives now and not waste one more minute."

"I've already told the justice of the peace to come over at five tonight, and we'll tie the knot as the sun goes down at 5:57." He smiled. "Unless you would like to wait until tomorrow morning."

She pressed her lips against his and whispered, "Mr. Chadwick, that is out of the question." She went on, her mouth still against his. "You planned this before our little scare, didn't you?"

Holding her even closer, Barry replied, "From now on, all our conversations should be conducted like this." He kissed her. Still holding her in his arms, he continued, "I spoke with Mrs. Adams this morning, and she is taking care of everything. Nell and Holt are coming over to stand up for us. And we'll have our honeymoon in our bedroom. By the way, you'd better do something about those red eyes of yours, or Nell and Holt will accuse me of beating you."

"Good point. The last thing I want to do is show up for our wedding looking like I ran into a truck."

From the minute they walked into the house, time accelerated. A quick swim in the pool, a short nap, a chance to change, and then Nell and Holt arrived with the justice of the peace. The ceremony was followed with a champagne toast. Mrs. Adams and Luis served the wedding supper to the Chadwicks and the Porters. Then everyone was gone—and it wasn't even nine in the evening.

"Well, Mrs. Chadwick, do you think we've had enough excitement for one day?"

"Mr. Chadwick, from the moment we got engaged, the excitement hasn't stopped. Would you mind very much if we could just have some peace and quiet?"

"Follow me to peace and quiet." They headed to the bedroom that they would share.

In silence, they took each other in their arms, while their hearts raced in anticipation of their new lives together. They gave of themselves unselfishly, eagerly, and with tenderness. The heavens opened, and they shared their first glimpse of eternity, where their souls had been destined to meet. In each other's arms, they fell asleep, content that they were at last one—now and forever. They felt blessed.

When they finally awoke, it was late morning, and the sun was shining. They felt like two floating clouds as they lay wrapped around each other.

"You know," Barry said, "we have to do this more often, Mrs. Chadwick."

"I'll mark your name down in my appointment book. Or you can call my secretary."

"I'll make it easy for you. Just sign me up forever."

"I see that I'm free for the next forever, so the time is yours."

"Merry—I love to say your name—Merry, have I told you how much I love you?"

"Tell me now. It's a different time."

"I love you."

"And I love you too. Let's always be in love like this. I'm so thankful that everything turned out okay."

"You're my wife. And for me, that's more than okay."

"Guess what? I'm hungry."

"For what?"

They both laughed and snuggled under the covers.

The Nassau trip was postponed, but with nothing to do but relax and enjoy each other, the honeymoon week sped by. Neither of them was aware of the passage of time, and by the end of the week, they were well on their way to knowing each other as true friends, soul mates, and confidants. The time together fused them in a way that was not immediately apparent to them, but they had begun the transformation that would bring them closer than ever.

Then the week was over, and they found themselves once more in the office of Dr. Singh. "I hope you had a pleasant week together," he said. "And I hope you did not do any running around. Did you rest as I prescribed?"

"Aside from it being our honeymoon," Barry said, "yes, we took it easy. Most of the time." He looked at Merry, who was attempting to suppress a smile.

"Good. That's what I wanted to hear. Then I take it you have had no recurrences of headaches or dizzy spells?"

"No. None. I feel rested and relaxed."

"Yes, that's what I thought would happen. After studying all your tests, we've concluded that you've been burning the candle at both ends. You're not twenty years old anymore. You don't need to be overly careful, but don't try to live a lifetime in one week."

"Then Barry is all right?" Merry asked.

"Sound as can be. The tests were all negative. But as I said, he just needs to remember he's not twenty and stop trying to do too much at once."

"Then we can go on the honeymoon trip we planned to Nassau," Barry said. "Can I go back to work?"

"I don't see why not. Just remember what I said, and you won't be coming back here anytime soon."

"So that's it?" Merry asked. "We can go?"

"Please do. I need to see my next patient. And much happiness to both of you."

Once outside, Merry and Barry sighed in mutual relief. Before they were halfway home, Barry embarked on a serious discussion about their future.

"I think I'd like to cut back and share some respon-sibilities of the company with you. Contracting is just one part of the whole picture. That way, you would know what's going on, and you would be able to use your talents. Are you interested?"

"Of course I'm interested. But I don't know anything about your businesses. Wouldn't I need a lot of training?"

"Yes, you would, but you'll catch on. I'll help you, and so will everyone else at Chadwick Enterprises."

"When do we start?"

"As soon as we get back from our official honey-moon—which starts exactly now."

"Maybe I should call my friends and let them know I am really married."

"Do it when we get back from our cruise. That way, you'll have something interesting to talk about."

"Believe me when I tell you that I have no intentions of giving those details to anyone."

"And what details might those be?"

"That's for you to find out."

By the second week of their honeymoon cruise, Barry and Merry had become a part of each other, singing their life songs and gaining a deeper understanding of their union. Long-past events that had simmered in Merry's consciousness had finally disappeared, releasing her from tending the burden of her unalterable past. She was free—because she finally belonged to Barry, and he belonged to her.

At last, she was in the parade of life and not a spectator.

Forty-Two

"What are you thinking about?" Barry looked over his sunglasses at Merry, who was lounging on a deck chair, absorbed in note taking.

"Remember when you asked me if I would take part in your work? I've been giving it a great deal of thought."

"And?"

"As soon as I finish decorating Chadwick Farms, I'd like to discuss a project that I think might be something new in homebuilding."

"Why not talk about it now?"

"All right. I was thinking it might be profitable to build a tract of small homes in West Palm Beach. Houses that don't look like they came out of a cookie cutter."

"Go on; tell me more."

"These houses would all be small, but what would separate them from the other small houses is that they'd be miniature adaptations of local mansions. These houses would be between twelve hundred and eighteen hundred square feet. And instead of their all being flat in the back, with uniform screened-in enclosures, they would have loggias and solariums and swimming pools. And they wouldn't all be lined up on the street like building blocks. They would be in a series of cul-de-sacs on winding streets. No golf courses, communal swimming pools, or tennis courts. Lots of landscaping—and furniture packages."

"Anything else?"

"This is just an idea."

"When we get home, we can work with our architects on this. We have a great tract that might lend itself to small but elegant houses. It would be a novel idea around here. We'll call them Merry Mansions."

"Then, you like?"

"I like. Now, would you care to accompany me to our stateroom? There's something I want to discuss with you."

Forty-Three

The plans Merry had discussed with Barry on their honeymoon became a reality. Within six months, five model homes were ready for viewing. The feature article in the real-estate section of the Sunday paper praised the homes as "the perfect palace at the perfect price. These homes are distinguished by the absence of synthetic materials. Each home features genuine decorative wood moldings. Bathrooms are offered in a choice of colors and exotic woods. Imported tile and marble are standard. The homes are scaled down in size, but not in quality." Thirty-five homes were sold in the first week, and the Chadwicks added another dimension to their relationship: as coworkers and business partners.

From the start, the project was an overwhelming success. When Barry suggested that the homes in Phase Two resemble the small houses on the Palm Beach historic trail, the Chadwick architects produced blueprints and scale models for what Barry named Pioneer Pointe. Construction would start just before Christmas.

Their days were filled with construction site visits, meetings with prospective buyers, and eating on the run. Merry was amazed at her weight gain. *Obviously,* she thought, *a burger a day and a chocolate drink will cause your hips to grow and your clothes to shrink.* She had her former supplier make up some pillows with the slogan, and she sent the samples off to Reno. Charles and Edward, who now managed the Manhattan studio, couldn't keep up with the orders.

Merry's working relationship with Reno continued with the interior design of Merry Mansions and Pioneer Pointe. Everything had fallen into place, except that she was feeling the effects of all her running around. By the autumn, she felt continually tired, bloated, and upset from the gastronomic garbage she consumed.

"I get so tired lately," she said to Barry, as they sat in their construction site office, eating Chinese takeout for lunch. "I think these crazy hours and junk food are finally catching up with me."

"We should ask Mrs. Adams to make us picnic lunches, but this lo mein is really good." Barry offered the box of noodles to her.

"No, thanks. I really don't feel well."

"Do you want to go home and rest?"

"I think I'd better. I really feel sick."

"Come on; let's go home."

For the rest of the afternoon, Merry felt horrible and vowed she would never so much as look at an egg roll again.

"I think you should see Dr. Van Allen," Barry said. "You might have food poisoning. I'll call him now."

"Okay. This is really awful."

Dr. Van Allen agreed to see her within the hour. When he had completed his examination, he smiled, "Well, Merry, it's not an egg roll that's causing you this discomfort. You don't have food poisoning; you're pregnant. Congratulations. Let's get Barry in here and tell him the good news."

"Are you sure I'm really...?" She couldn't even utter the word *pregnant*.

"You are. Now, let's get Barry."

When Barry heard the news, tears of joy streamed down his glowing face. "Oh, Merry, this is so wonderful. We're going to be a family." Putting his arms around her, he kissed her and said, "Thank you, my love."

Dr. Van Allen became serious. "Would you mind if we continue this conversation before you two get overly involved?" They all laughed, and Dr. Van Allen said, "I want you to make an appointment to get the rest of your tests. Now, go home and celebrate with lemonade. Once you get on the mommy wagon, you won't be drinking until you get to the station."

"Let's go home," Barry said, "and tomorrow we'll have the wagon make a couple of stops. Nursery room shopping."

She grinned. "As the conductor said, 'All aboard.'"

Once settled in the back seat of the Silver Shadow, Merry snuggled in the crook of Barry's arm. As they rounded Sloane's Curve, she pulled a small white envelope of confetti from her purse, the same confetti that she had scooped up from the floor of her apartment on that gloomy day of her forty-second birthday. It seemed so long ago. She opened the window and released the tiny bits of colored paper. As the confetti streamed out the window, she nestled deeper into Barry's arms and closed her eyes. Mrs. Merry Chadwick was going home.

Barbara Shorr

Barbara (Bobbi) received an associate's degree from Hartford College for Women, where she studied creative writing with Prof. Oliver Butterworth. She subsequently earned a bachelor's degree from the University of Connecticut and master's degree in art education from Central Connecticut State University. She served as a senior docent at the Wadsworth Atheneum Museum of Art in Hartford and a senior docent at the Norton Museum of Art in West Palm Beach.

Barbara and husband, Bernard, lived most of their married life in Avon, Connecticut and now reside in Wellington, Florida with Sweet Pea, their cat.

Barbara is a member of the Palm Beach Writers Group. *Mansion Dreams* is her first novel.